LUNA & ANDRES

A DARK CAPTIVE ROMANCE

NIKITA SLATER

LUNA & ANDRES derives from **Anita Gray's** International Bestselling, **The Dark Romance Series.**

Blaire is "Compelling Dark Romance," says Anna Zaires, New York Times Bestselling Author

"Screen worthy," says the BestSellers & BestStellars Book Blog

All titles in **The Dark Romance Series** are available with Kindle Unlimited and as Audiobooks.

To find out more, *Click Here*

PROLOGUE

ANDRES

Warmth hits my veins like sex after a long, agonizing dry spell. I take a breath, feeling the air rush through my lungs. Is it my imagination or is the air newer, fresher than the dank shit that was in here only moments ago? I sip at it like a man starving and lean back in the lounge chair, draping my arms over the side. I look at my left arm, at the needle sticking straight out from the vein. I think about reaching over to flick the used needle away, but my eyes catch on the tattoos surrounding the metal prick.

Luna.

Her name is a swirl of colour in the bleak wasteland of cartel tats that proclaim my place, my superiority within the organization run by family. Los Zetas. The most feared cartel in Mexico and beyond. And I am among the elite within this vast army of underworld thugs. These marks upon my body are trophies of war, my right of passage. Lost innocence. Except for Luna. The one mark I had written over and over; on my arms, my legs, my neck and over my heart. My salvation.

She gives me the strength to reach out and take the needle between my fingers, now shaky from the drug flowing freely, blissfully through my system. I pull the metal from my arm and toss it away, uncaring where it lands. I settle back into the chair with a sigh and close my eyes, picturing her behind my lids. Her soft skin, that long, flowing mane, that luscious, curvy, utterly fuckable body.

I wanted her from the first moment I saw her, standing over some stupid, mouthy cunt in a bar, her fist pulled back, a broken bottle held high, about to disfigure the other woman for life, if not kill her. I couldn't look away. She was a warrior, a witch, the most gorgeous woman I'd ever seen in that hell hole Mexican town. Now she belongs to me. My Luna, my pretty baby. The thing that keeps me sane.

Guilt starts to eat away at my high, tearing an ugly hole in the euphoria I've worked so hard to achieve. I know I need to push her away, shove my Luna to another place where she's safe from all this evil bullshit. So fucking hard though. She's been my everything for three years. I dragged her out of that poverty-stricken shithole and set her up on a pedestal where she can shine like the queen she is meant to be. My Luna, my love.

Unbidden, her beautiful face floats through my drug hazed mind. I smile and reach for her, but she disappears. She disapproves. She hates the shit I pump into my veins, pretends she doesn't know where I go for weeks on end, showing up eventually like a lost wolf, sick, starved and shivering, half the man I used to be. Shame eating at my insides, withdrawal eating away everything else.

I blink and look up, see her in front of me. I frown; this isn't her. She's at home, safe in our bed, probably worried. She knows, but she doesn't want to know. So she goes on without me when I disappear. We call it business, even though she's wise enough to know when I'm actually away on Los Zetas work. She's not stupid. She'll protect me and my reputation with her life.

"You can't be here," I whisper to her ghost, stumbling to my feet.

She looks at me, looks through me. As though I don't exist. Anger courses through my veins, speeding the drug. I shake my head bringing a hand up to center myself. I know I'm stumbling, swaying, should probably sit back down. But I need to send my pregnant wife back home, where she'll be safe.

"Get the fuck out of here," I snarl, swiping at her.

I immediately regret the action. I don't want to hurt her. Fuck, I never wanted to hurt my Luna. Yet every time I leave her, leave to destroy these demons, immerse myself in the darkness so I won't take it home, I know I'm stabbing her in the heart all over again. Those dark, bottomless eyes tell me of her love and pain each time I walk out the door with no intention of coming back until I've purged. Why the fuck did she have to come into my life? My greatest comfort, my worst shame.

I collapse to my knees at her feet, unable to remain standing in a room that won't stop spinning. I laugh wildly and reach for her, missing. "Stand still, esposa," I demand, shouting at the mirage as it shimmers and dances out of reach.

I continue to kneel at her feet, completely in awe of my glorious wife. Her body is full and round, pregnant with our second child. Tears rush to my eyes as I realize what I've done. Once more I have left my Luna, my wife, as she is so close to giving birth. I've been in this shack, shooting heroin into my veins for six days. It'll take weeks of agonizing pain, and nightmarish withdrawals before I'm fit to go home again. She could give birth before I'm once more able to be with her. And she may not want me. Not that it matters. She'll take me, regardless of her feelings, regardless of the state I'm in.

For better or worse.

It was for Luna that I came here. To purge the black from my soul. That last job was a sick fucking piece of work. The death of our enemy and his family had not been smooth or easy; like art, the passing of their regime had painted the walls in abstract. I had been placed in charge of the takeover and subsequent cleanup. A big job. One that had made my family proud.

It also called to the beast in me. A bleak, dark creature that constantly tries to claw its way out. A thing that can't be calmed by anything, not even my Luna. The only thing that suppresses the beast, the darkness, is heroin. My escape.

I pull my gun from my holster, surprised it's still there after so many hours, so many days, lurching in and out of my own mind. I hadn't even bothered changing my clothes after the takeover. Simply picked up and left, instructing my men to finish the cleanup. I knew if I didn't leave I would do something truly regrettable.

I look up at the devastating lovely vision before me and slowly raise the gun, pointing it at her head. Even drugged out of my mind, I know my aim is good. "Be a good girl and go home, Luna," I whisper. I pull the trigger. The shot echoes through the room, deafening me. I drop the gun and hunch over the floor, knowing I'm about to take my last trip. I can't do this again. Can't do it to my wife, my children, my sanity. I need to find a new way to release my demons.

I sink my nails into the dusty wooden floor and scrape them toward me, hoping to feel something, at the same time wanting the numbness I came for.

I look up, desperate for one last glimpse of my salvation, but she's gone, banished. I sit back on my haunches and contemplate the next few weeks. Pain. I've been shot, stabbed, kicked in the balls. Nothing compares to heroin withdrawal. The horrific, sickening pain will let me know that I'm still alive. Still a man, a husband, a father.

"Wait for me, Luna," I whisper, collapsing until I'm sitting on the floor with my back against the chair behind me. "I'm coming home, cariño."

1

LUNA

Two years later

"Mama, when are we going home?"

I stop, my hand on the light switch. I take a breath and look over my shoulder at my four-year-old son, such a miniature replica of his father that my heart aches. Except this time, instead of a happy ache I feel an agonizing wrench. I blink back the tears, not wanting him to see my distress, and try to find my voice.

"We might stay here for a while, cariño," I tell him, keeping my voice steady. "I'm not sure yet." *It depends on whether or not your papá can find us.*

I go back to the bed and give him an extra kiss, pressing his small body against mine, absorbing his warmth and taking in his unique babyish scent, grateful he hasn't lost it yet. Soon he'll be bigger, will not want his mama to hold him so close and embarrass him with affection. Then I will have to settle for showering his younger sister with my love. I press my lips against his forehead and help him snuggle back under the blankets.

"I miss papá," he says sleepily, smothering a yawn against his pillow.

"I know, baby," I whisper, smoothing the hair back on his head.

"Why couldn't he come to Cuba with us?" His sooty black lashes blink up at me and for a moment I think I see accusation in those too-serious crystal blue eyes. He's so much like his father I don't know what I'll do with him in a few years. Cristo is the main reason I made the decision to leave. I couldn't abide the thought of this beautiful child becoming the dark, twisted anger-fueled man his father has become.

The tears rush to the surface again as I contemplate a life without my Andres. It's too bleak for words, yet it has become my chosen existence. I stand up and turn away. "He's too busy working," I say shortly. "Go to sleep."

I leave the room and go next door to check on Sola. My baby daughter is sound asleep in her crib, her fine black curls fuzzed out around her small head in a halo. She's wearing a tiny purple jumper with the feet attached. I run my finger down her cheek, marvelling, as I always do, at the incredible softness. This little beauty stole my heart the moment she left my womb two years ago. She's been a demanding little diva ever since, wrapping the men in her life around that tiny little finger. I pull her blanket up and kiss my fingertips pressing them against her tiny lips. I wish I could press my lips against her, inhale her scent, but I'm too short to bend that far over her crib.

I leave the bedroom with a sigh of regret and wander down the hall toward the kitchen area. The house is modest but comfortable. I chose it because I was able to pay cash without raising suspicion. No one will question a Latina woman with children, settling into a small home on the outskirts of Havana; a bustling city with plenty of action but no one to mind my business. At least that's what I'm hoping.

"You okay?" Pedro's deep voice draws my attention and I glance toward him.

He's standing in the back door, smoking a cigarette, blowing the stream of smoke out into the night. I wrinkle my nose in annoyance. I hate when people smoke around my children or even in the same home as my children. Pedro knows that this behaviour is borderline unacceptable, but he also knows I can't complain much. I have no one else to protect me, no one else that would have left the Los Zetas organizations with the wife of a Decena. He knew it was suicide and still he came.

I know why. Pedro wants me. He's always wanted me. Fortunately for his health he was good at keeping his lustful thoughts to himself. If my husband had ever caught wind, Pedro would have begged for death long before Andres would've granted it. Instead, Pedro managed to place himself in a trusted position within the household as one of my personal bodyguard's. A position that I shamelessly used in my bid for freedom.

"What do you mean?" I ask coolly, flattening my gaze as I stare past him. Long years as a cartel wife have taught me how to keep my emotions to myself.

"You left your husband and your home," he says, taking another drag, this time not bothering to blow the stream outside. "They'll come after you. No telling what he'll do when he finds you. You must be upset."

My eyes settled on him, letting him know just how much of a cockroach I think he is. This man is far too beneath me to be speaking in such a familiar manner. It doesn't matter that he helped get me and my children out of Mexico. We both know how he expects to get paid. "You don't know me,"

I finally say, my voice dripping with ice. "And you don't know my husband if you think you can predict his actions. You will not speak to me of this again."

He holds his hands up as though surrendering and says, "My apologies Señora Decena. I only wanted to help."

"I will tell you when I require your assistance," I snap, slamming a teacup onto the counter and setting the pot to boil. At least this place comes with a few of the essential amenities. "For now, you are dismissed."

I can feel his hesitation, can feel his brain working. He knows there is very little stopping him from simply taking what he wants. Taking what he came here for. My hands sneak around to the front of my bathrobe and tighten the knot below the counter where he can't see, a useless gesture if he attacks.

"Goodnight," he grunts and turns away, leaving through the open door and closing it behind him. There is a small shack on the property that I told him to stay in. I stare after him at the dark window, still shaken. What am I going to do about him if he gets serious?

I jump as the kettle starts whistling on the stovetop. Heart pounding in my chest I turn to take it off the heat and pour the hot water over my teabag. The soothing smell of chamomile teases my senses and helps to calm me. I take my cup to the table and slide onto the padded chair, setting my cup on the scarred table. Somehow this small, humble house calms me, despite the shabbiness. It reminds me of my home growing up, of mama. Her image comes unbidden to my mind. I smile at the bittersweet thought. My mama was strict, hard-working and crankier than a basket full of scorpions. But she was mine and she loved me.

I take a sip of the hot tea allowing the heat to help settle my nerves. I laugh a little. There's no way to settle my nerves now. I'm going to be a nervous wreck, looking over my shoulder for the rest of my, probably short, life. My husband is going to see this as the worst kind of betrayal. And it is. I've done what I threatened so many times to do. I've left him. But I haven't just left him, I've taken his children with me. The first is unforgivable, the second is a death sentence. He won't have a choice. His family will insist that he hunt and destroy the woman who stole his legacy.

A shudder ripples through me and I try to shove such a grim thought to the back of my mind. I made my plan, executed it and now I must follow through. There can be no going back.

A loud ringing sound crashes through my musing, startling me. My fingers shake the teacup splashing hot water over my hand. I cry out and leap up from the chair, rushing to the stove to snatch up the cloth hanging there. I press it against my hand and gulp deep breaths in. It's not the burn that's upsetting me though. It's the phone, sitting on the counter where I left it. My emergency cell. The last connection I have to Andres.

I knew he would call, and I knew that this moment would come. That I would only be able to answer this phone once. The ringing stops before I can pick up. But I know my husband. He's a persistent bastard. He has now returned home to an empty house, no family, no note. He will give me this one opportunity to explain before he starts tearing the world up to find us.

I take the three steps that bring me to the counter and stare down at the silver phone. Untraceable he once told me. In case there was ever a threat to the family and I needed to disappear. I was to take this phone so Andres could connect when it was safe to do so. He never imagined he would be calling the phone for this reason.

It starts ringing again and I reach out with trembling fingers, wincing as pain from the burn shoots through my wrist. I feel dizzy at the coming confrontation. I pick up the phone, press the little green button and set it against my ear. "Andres," I whisper, my voice weak and wobbly to my ears.

"You're safe?" he demands.

"Yes," I reply, trying to ignore the guilt eating at the edges of my consciousness. Of course the first thing my husband would want to know is if I am hurt. "And the children, we're all safe."

"Then where the fuck are you?" he explodes, he deep voice echoing through the line.

I wince, holding the phone slightly away. I picture him standing in our beautiful home in Mexico, on Los Zetas territory, at The Site. He would be alone, confused, justifiably angry. But I'm also angry. And I am done. I can't survive this marriage anymore, never knowing if he's going to come home or if he's going to allow the darkness to finally take him. Or if an enemy has finally murdered the man I love. But most of all, I refuse to agonize over the years to come, the unimaginable pain we'll be causing our children.

"I can't tell you," I say, trying to infuse some strength into my words.

There's a moment of silence. I hold my breath and wait, not quite knowing what to expect. Andres can be a terribly violent man, but he shelters me from the worst. I've rarely had reason to glimpse the savage I know is buried within my husband, the man that emerges when he goes to work for the cartel. I can feel tension leaping down the line from him to me as his swift brain works out my cryptic words.

"Why the fuck not, Luna?" he finally snarls.

My fingers tighten around the phone until they stiffen. My knees buckle and I slide to the floor, my back against the counter. I wrap my free arm around my legs and stare unseeing at the wall opposite. I curl my toes against the cheap linoleum.

"You didn't come home when you were supposed to," I say, choking a little as I remember pacing and worrying, wondering if he'd been killed on his last assignment. Then his men came back home without him, his second-in-command explaining to me that he's decided to stay behind for a few more weeks. I knew what that meant.

"I didn't come home," Andres repeated, his voice a deep growl. "So you decided to leave? Is this your way of getting attention? Is that what this is, Luna? Because if it is, then you can get your ass home now and we can discuss this, like the fucking adult you are."

"I-it's not about attention, Andres," I stumble to get the words out. The heat of his anger stabs at me, even over the vast distance of the Caribbean ocean. I lick my lips and swipe a finger under my eyelids, catching the moisture.

"Then what, Luna? Make me fucking understand," he snarls.

A shaft of pain slices through me at his tone of voice. He never speaks this way to me. I press a hand against my chest and lie. "You didn't come back with your men from P-panama, Andres. You just disappeared for weeks after. For all I knew it was another woman, or... or drugs again. What am I supposed to think?"

"That's garbage and you know it, Luna!" he roars. "You are supposed to trust me. You are supposed to stay where I tell you, keep my home for me. Not kidnap my kids and leave because you think I'm doing something you don't like. You stupid little bitch."

I flinch under the onslaught of his anger. This was the side of my husband I knew I would have to face, the terrifying reality I'd spent years avoiding. "I'm sorry," I whisper.

"If you were sorry, you would come home," he grits out.

"I can't do that," I reply, my voice unsteady. "I don't trust that you didn't use heroin. I don't believe that you can contain this evil and I don't want my children around it. I've seen what it does and it frightens me."

He says nothing for a moment, but his seething rage comes through loud and clear. I shove a shaking hand through my hair, wishing I had a cigarette to help calm me. I suppose I could ask Pedro, but the consequences of seeking him out might be more than I'm willing to deal with.

Andres tries to soften his voice when he speaks again. "This is ridiculous, Luna. Just tell me where you are. I'll come get you and we can talk about this when you and our children are safe at home again. This is a marriage, one that you agreed to willingly. You don't get to just walk away because you don't like something."

I laugh bitterly. Yes, I'd agreed to the marriage, but Andres wouldn't have let me escape him, even if I hadn't been willing. Once he set his sights on me there was no going back to my old life. What a naïve child I was. Well, I'm grown up now and I'm not willing to compromise. Not on this.

"No, Andres. This is too important to me." My voice catches as I think of the many nights I sat up waiting for Andres to walk through the door, disappointment my cold companion when morning lit the sky and my husband had not returned. "We won't be coming home, not to a husband and father that is unstable."

"That's not your choice!" he yells.

My heart thunders in my chest, feeling as though it will claw its way up my throat and right out of my mouth.

Andres' anger is fearsome and I hate that I'm on the receiving end. I take a few calming breaths. I can hear that he is doing the same.

"Actually," I say in a much calmer voice, "it is my choice now. I have removed my children from the danger."

Heavy silence fills the line. I can hear the ticking of a clock and glance toward it. It's old-fashioned, like so many things in Cuba. I love it here, which is part of the reason I chose Cuba as an escape. It's also relatively easy to hide out.

"You are going to think hard about this now, baby, because your response to my questions will determine your future. Where the fuck did you take my children?" he demands, the hard edge to his voice razor sharp. "Tell me now and I will keep this between us. If you resist, then it becomes Los Zetas business."

We both know what that means. Once my disappearance is known to his family there is nothing he can do to save me. They will demand my blood. A sob catches in my throat and I feel myself weakening. Andres is the only man I have ever loved. He is my lover and my protector. Leaving him went against my every instinct. But I still believe it was the right thing to do.

"No, Andres," I whisper.

I hear something shatter in the background and wonder what he's broken. I decorated our house, painstakingly chose all of the beautiful, expensive furnishings. Lovely knickknacks that have very little use, but that I value anyway because I grew up destitute, in a home where all our money had to go to food and shelter. I hadn't intended that I would ever see my house again, but the thought of my husband breaking up the contents of our home still hurts. Poetic, I suppose, since I'm breaking up his family.

"Then we have nothing else to say to each other," he tells me after bringing himself back under control.

"I love you, Andres."

"I will find you, Luna," he says, his voice low and lethal. "God help you."

The line goes dead. I sit with the phone still cradled against my ear. A cold shiver slides down my spine and the phone drops into my lap. I finally allow the tears to fall, slipping warm and wet down my cheeks. I drop my face against my knees and sob for the first time since taking my children and walking away from my marriage.

God help me.

2

ANDRES

Betrayal churns in my gut as I stare down at the phone, disbelief still my strongest emotion. How is it possible that Luna, my rock, my only love, could leave me? Not just leave but take my children with her. Fury wells up once more. I pick up the phone and hurl it, uncaring that it smashes against our stainless steel refrigerator and falls to the floor in pieces. I know Luna well enough to know that she won't answer the sister phone again. She's said her piece, explained her betrayal. Weak as it was.

My fingers clench into fists and I know if she were standing in front of me I would snap her neck without a shred of remorse. I would tear her body to pieces with my bare hands and feed her to the dogs. I've spent years defending her selfish, reckless behaviours. But this... this cannot be explained away. This will be her final act. If she is running away because she fears the darkness, the monster, then she better be ready, because she's seen nothing yet. When I get my hands on her, she will beg for a swift death.

And I will smile at my bitch of a wife while denying her request. She will live just long enough to regret leaving me.

With a roar I turn and throw my fist through the sliding glass door. I can feel the flesh split on my knuckles as the satisfying sound of glass shatters the silence. Still the anger rides high, the black stain that I can never fully get rid of urges me to do further damage, to tear apart the home that my wife built for us. It's a false home anyway, built on false promises.

I pick up one of her favourite vases and hurl it at a window, adrenaline coursing through me as I watch my refection shatter. I don't stop until I've broken everything within reach, stalking through the first floor of our house throwing, smashing and tearing everything within sight. It helps relieve some of the terrible rage that boils up.

"Everything alright?"

I pull my gun and turn on the spot, my finger twitching against the trigger. If anyone except Alberto had been standing there they would've been dead. "Get the fuck out," I growl, slamming my gun on the counter.

He holds his hands up but doesn't leave. "Can I do anything?" he asks, as though asking in a different way might get him a different answer.

I open my mouth to tell him to go fuck himself, but then I stop. I need him. Alberto is the only man within the cartel that is entirely loyal to me. Who won't go to Charlie, my brother, my boss, if I ask him for complete secrecy. And though I want to tear her treacherous heart out, I want to do it in my own time, in my own way, without the demands and influence of my family.

I nod once and wave him to a chair. Striding over broken glass, uncaring of the damage I'm doing to the floor, I grab a bottle of tequila and two shot glasses. I sit with Alberto, setting the bottle in front of him and waving at him to pour. He unscrews the cap and splashes a healthy shot of the clear liquid into each glass. Without pause I toss mine back, savouring the burn as it hits the back of my throat and warms my stomach.

I set my glass on the table and nod for another pour. He obliges and this time takes his shot with me. Once our glasses are back on the table, I speak. "Luna has taken my children and left."

I can see a quick flash of surprise before Alberto manages to smother the emotion. He knows better than to have any kind of opinion, even a silent one. Unsolicited opinions within our organization can be deadly. He inclines his head and pours another splash of liquor into each glass. "She is on vacation?" he ventures. "Shopping perhaps."

We both know that this is not true. "Sí, she is shopping," I grunt my acknowledgment of the lie.

"We will find out where she is shopping so you can join her," he continues, his agile brain working faster than mine. This is why I need Alberto on my side. I'm too caught up in emotion. I want to find her, strangle her, fuck her, beat her. But I won't be able to do any of that if I can't get my hands on her.

"Yes, we must find her," I agree. "Bring my children home."

3

LUNA

It's been three days since my conversation with Andres. I try to settle into a routine with the children, try to show them the Havana that I love, but I can't help but look over my shoulder every five minutes. If I'm honest with myself, I know it's just a matter of time before Andres finds me. He has connections, he has motivation and he won't stop until his children are safe at the Los Zetas site once more. And I'm punished for daring to remove them, and myself, from his life.

I adjust my oversize sunglasses and glance around surreptitiously. We're visiting the Plaza Vieja in Old Havana. Nothing compares to the old cobbled streets and restored buildings of Old Havana. Although Sola is still too young to appreciate the sights, Cristo is intelligent and I want my children to soak up as much history as possible. Perhaps come to understand both the allure and the harm of a regime under a dictatorship. No one suspicious catches my eye. Except for Pedro. That asshole has been trailing us everywhere, even when I tell him to stay behind. I give him the evil eye and clutch my daughter harder against my chest.

"I can take her if she she's getting too heavy for you, Luna," he drawls, looking down my cleavage where Sola has grabbed onto my peach blouse and pulled it to one side.

I try to delicately pull the material from her small fingers and rebutton it without drawing too much notice. "That's Señora Decena to you," I snap coolly, holding his gleaming brown gaze. "And no, I can manage my children."

He holds my look for several long seconds before lifting an eyebrow and moving slightly away. My heart pounds. I know my outright hostility won't hold him for long. But God help me, I need this man. He has access to underworld contacts I don't, people and papers that will allow us to travel without discovery. The problem is, eventually he's going to demand payment, and it's not going to be money. If I'd had any other choices, any other men willing to betray my husband, I would have chosen them over Pedro in a heartbeat.

"Mama."

I look down as Cristo tugs on the edge of my shirt. I do my best to smile at him. "Yes, baby?" I ask brightly.

"Not a baby," he grumbles. "I'm hungry. Can we stop walking now?"

I sigh and stop walking, looking around to get my bearings in the square. Cuba isn't exactly known for its cuisine, but I've been to Havana a few times, and I know a couple of decent restaurants that will do. "Of course, Cristo." I shift Sola in my arms so she's sitting on a hip, one of my arms wrapped firmly around her. This frees up my other hand for Cristo. I reach for him, take his hand in mine and lead him out of the square toward a bistro only a few blocks away.

We wind our way through a marketplace, Cristo marvelling at all the bright colours and friendly locals trying to sell their wares. I smile, but move quickly past, promising my children that we will come back and look at the souvenirs later. I don't blame them for wanting something. We came to Cuba in a rush. Once my decision to leave Andres was made, we had to leave Mexico in a hurry with minimal baggage. I left most of the children's toys behind. Now the brightly patterned wooden trucks, license plates and dolls are appealing.

It takes only a few moments for us to be seated at the small bistro. The selection is limited, especially for children. A quick glance at the menu and I rattle off several items in Spanish. I flick a glance toward our unwanted companion, who has taken a seat across from me, unbidden. I don't order anything for him. He can fend for himself.

"Is papá coming today?" Cristo asks as I fuss with Sola's bib.

A shudder ripples down my spine and I ignore Pedro, whose eyes are boring into me. I run my fingers down Cristo's cheek and murmur, "Your father is busy, my darling. It's just us for now. We will have some fun though, travelling around and shopping. You will like that, hmm?"

Cristo's blazing blue eyes, sharp with intelligence, hold mine. He seems to look for something. He is only four yet he is so much older than his years, he always has been. As much as I've tried to make him my baby, he is more his father's child than mine. Sola, with her dramatic ways and her big dark eyes, is one hundred percent my child. A shaft of pure pain pierces me, stealing my breath. I know what I'm doing is correct, the right path, but it hurts so fucking bad.

There is no one on this planet that completes me except for the father of these children. And I walked away from him, turned my back on his home, knowing I could never go back. Tears glisten and I'm forced to glance away, into the malevolent gaze of Pedro. I narrow my eyes.

"Come, children, let's eat," I say as the food arrives. "Then we will go back to that marketplace and pick up a few souvenirs. Some toys for you to play with while we're on vacation."

Cristo grins and chatters about the brightly coloured trucks he saw and which one he might choose for himself while Sola grabs for a baked tortilla, shoving it in her mouth. Relief washes through me. Happy children are something that I recognize. Though serious, Cristo isn't used to hardship and the last thing I want to introduce him to is a life of poverty or pain; both things I'd experienced in spades as a child.

After a few purchases for the children in the marketplace, we finish our day in Old Havana with a visit to the Museo de la Ciudad. Exhausted but happy, we make our way back to the bungalow. Despite the unhappy circumstances surrounding our visit to Cuba, I somehow managed to make our day of sightseeing fun and educational. I'd also been able to push the pain of not having Andres with us to the side. He loves Cuba. He's the reason I know Havana well enough to come here.

I tell Pedro to stay out of the house as I unlock the door and usher the children inside. I slam it in his face and twist the lock, knowing that he could easily find his way in if he wants to. I place our purchases on the counter and hurry Cristo and Sola to their bedrooms at the end of the hall, urging them to change for the night. Instead of annoyance, I feel amusement as I listen to Sola's stumbles and Cristo's grumbles while they get ready for sleep. My son thinks he is too old now for such an early bedtime and my daughter is too clumsy to put her bedclothes on by herself. She usually has a nanny to help.

Ignoring the wrinkles to my expensive silk skirt, I go to my knees in front of her, a smile on my lips. "You need help, my love?" I ask gently.

"Sí, mama," she pouts, holding out an arm with a footsie pajama bottom on it.

I laugh, take it in my hand and tug. She goes flying back, landing on her diapered butt. I bite my lip to suppress my giggles until I see her reaction. She looks up at me with a suspicious frown marring her perfect forehead, her black eyes glowing retribution. "Mama..." she starts, her high-pitched voice on the edge of a tantrum.

"Wow, is that a unicorn?" I exclaim excitedly smoothing the pajamas out and pointing.

Her eyes flit over the top and she nods, reaching for it, her tiny fingers scrunching against the soft material. "Purple," she informs me seriously.

"Huh," I say, snapping the pajamas out and holding them up for her to step into. "I really thought it was more of a lilac."

She puts her hand on my shoulder and steps, first one leg in, wiggling her toes into the bottom. "No, mama," she insists. "Purple!"

I chuckle and help her with the other leg, pulling the arms on and zipping the pajamas up the front. Once she's changed I swing her up into my arms and carry her into the washroom where I help her brush her teeth. I supervise Cristo, who can brush his own teeth now, but won't without a parent or nanny around, then settle them both into bed with kisses and a story each. I'm a little surprised Sola isn't insisting on sleeping with her brother since she's in a strange house, but she seems to settle easily.

After the children are snuggled into bed I wander to the

kitchen to set the kettle to boil. I stare at it absently, my thoughts turning away from the innocence of my children. Though I desperately don't want to, I know I must seek out Pedro to discuss our next steps. We've been in Havana too long. We have to move, change locations if we are to have half a chance of surviving the Decenas.

I turn the stove element off and pour hot water over my teabag. I set the teacup aside, leaving it untouched for now. With a sigh of disgust I move to the back door, unlocking it and stepping out into the dark night. Acrid smoke immediately assails my nostrils, telling me that Pedro is stalking the yard. Though I hate the idea that he might have been watching me through the sliding glass door, I'm grateful that I don't have to seek him out in the confines of the small shack he inhabits.

"Pedro?" I say hesitantly. I may be able to smell him, but I can't see him. I pull my long, thick mane of hair off my neck and look around, searching the darkness.

I jump as he steps into the slight glow cast from the kitchen light.

"Señora Decena," he drawls.

My hackles rise immediately. Since our arrival in Cuba, every word out of this man's mouth has taken on a disrespectful tone. I want to verbally slap him in a way that only Luna Decena is capable of, but he's a half foot taller than me and probably outweighs me by fifty pounds of solid muscle. He's still half the man my husband is, but I'm not willing to spar with him, not when I could get hurt. It would leave my children vulnerable, without protection. I swallow my hatred and look away so he can't see the venom.

"We need to move," I say.

"Move?" he asks slowly.

I grit my teeth. He's playing with me. We discussed all

possibilities before we came to Cuba. He knows the plan, knows we won't be staying here long. "Yes," I say calmly. "We need to leave Cuba so Andres doesn't catch up to us."

He takes his time answering, though he knows we need to work out the details of our next move. I can hear music off in the distance. I try to work out if it's a live band or a radio. It's beautiful, uniquely Cuban. I sigh and cross my arms over my chest, rubbing at the bare flesh. I'm not cold, the evening is warm and humid. I'm sad, uncertain, fearful. Any number of emotions that I keep trying to suppress, but now that I'm getting tired from lack of sleep and nervousness, I'm beginning to fail at hiding it. I want to stay in Cuba, somewhere familiar, somewhere with happy memories, but I know I can't.

"France." His voice rumbles, cutting through the music.

I shudder and shake my head. Though I can barely make out his shadowy form in the darkness I know he can see me in the light filtering from the kitchen behind me. "No, France will be one of the first place the Decenas will look," I say, my voice barely above a whisper. I want to speak with strength, but there's nothing left in me. I've given up... for now. I'll find more after I sleep. I'll do it for my children. "I think... I think... maybe, Malaysia," I say, trying to get my exhausted mind to work. I know I should have worked this out ahead of time, but we departed Mexico so quickly, came to Cuba. It was probably stupid to come to a place that Andres knows and loves as much as I do, but I don't think he'll expect me to stay on this side of the ocean.

"You think," Pedro says derisively.

I stand up straighter and glare in his direction. "I know," I snap, turning my back on him and reaching for the door. "We leave for Kuala Lumpur tomorrow. Make the arrangements."

I feel proud of myself. Now I'm starting to sound like Luna Decena again. Self-assured, in control and a little spoiled. I open the door but before I can step inside Pedro grabs my arm, swings me around and pushes me back against the glass. I open my mouth to protest but he covers my mouth with his, shoving his tongue inside. I freeze, instantly afraid. All thought flees and I'm helpless against his onslaught as his hands snake over my body, squeezing and pressing.

I'm terrified that he's going to drag me to the ground and rape me right there in the back yard of our rental cottage. Tears prick my eyes and still I can't move. I choke and cough into his mouth, the feel of his slimy tongue causing me to gag. The tiny involuntary resistance is enough to make him stop for a moment. He lifts his head and glares down at me. I can see him now as he stands over me, his face an ugly lust-filled mask.

I want to scream and fight and claw him to pieces. An image of Blaire races through my sluggish brain. I know exactly what she would do. If Pedro had dared to touch her in such a way she would have murdered him with such violence that he would've been unrecognizable by the time she was done. I desperately wish I had even a little of her skill. Instead I'm as frozen as a statue, as weak as a kitten when threatened by a man like this. Pathetic. I'd done more damage in my youth when Marta Sanchez had called my mother a whore. But this is different...

"You thought my services were free?" Pedro groans, turning my head to the side so he can slobber on my ear and neck.

I frantically try to get my brain moving, try to tell myself to lie to him. I can deal with him later. Anything is better than what he wants from me. I do my best to channel my mother, one of the best actresses I knew. I suck back the sobs that threaten my composure, blink back the tears and find my voice.

"I'm well aware of your wants, Pedro," I say coolly, allowing a small purr of enticement to my voice. "But I've just left my husband, the Zetas are most likely hunting us and my children are only one room over. I'm really not in the mood... cariño."

His erection presses excitedly against my hip and I close my eyes, trying to mask my shudder of repulsion as a shiver. He runs a hand down my arm and I'm forced to grit my teeth. "You can come to my shack, chica. We can have a good time over there and your children will never hear."

I want to scream at this motherfucker and then slap myself silly for ever enlisting his services. Then again, I would never have escaped safely if I'd asked anyone else. I remind myself once more, Pedro had the connections and was the only man who wouldn't immediately turn me over to my husband. I swallow the bile threatening to rise in my throat, turn the fakest of smiles up at him and say, "It will be so much better if I'm not worried about my babies waking up and looking for me." When he opens his mouth to protest I place my hand against his chest and run it down to his belly in one smooth, erotic motion. "Trust me, darling, we will make love very soon and it will be more than you ever hoped for."

He groans out loud and places a palm at the back of my head, crushing me against him in a hug. I can feel his heart beating against my cheek. This time I can't hold back the tears. I miss my husband, *his* warmth, the sound of *his* heart beating. Not this maniac. I mumble a goodnight and turn away, rushing through the back door. I slam it shut behind me and lock it. Of course he is well able to come through that door if he wants to. He might be disgusting but he isn't stupid.

I walk mechanically to my teacup, pick it up and lift it to my lips. It's cooled down now, more than I'm willing to drink. A sob bursts from my lips and I hurl the cup toward the sink, feeling slightly better at the satisfying sound of shattering glass. I shut the light off and go to bed, checking on the children as I go.

4

ANDRES

I don't often smoke, but the occasion seems to call for it and Pedro is kind enough to leave a pack and a lighter out for me. Since I quit using heroin my cravings for other substances has increased; the need to take myself out of certain situations paramount. This isn't one of those situations. I want to be here, in the moment, enjoying every moan of pain, every drop of blood spilled. This man will learn what happens when my family is taken from me. Unfortunately, he won't live long enough to tell others not to fuck with me and mine.

I inhale deeply, savouring the sensation as it fills my lungs, burning in the way only an ex-smoker can appreciate. I'm sitting in a chair, in the corner of his room. I haven't bothered to be quiet, but he still hasn't woken, the man who has betrayed me. This annoys me. If a man must go to his death he should wake up and do it on his feet, face me like a man. I stub the cigarette out in the ashtray and stand. I flip the light on and approach the bed, giving it a kick for good measure.

Finally, Pedro gives me the response I desire, groaning

and turning over to face me. I grin at him, letting my presence sink in for a moment. The second recognition hits, I let my fist fly, shattering his nose where he lays in his bed. His head flies to the side and blood sprays across the pillow and up the wall next to the bed. I take a fistful of his hair and drag him from the small bed onto the floor. He's almost completely naked, except for a pair of worn boxer briefs.

"Pedro, my friend," I laugh down at him like we're old buddies, dropping him at my feet. When he tries to push himself backwards enough to gain his feet, I kick him hard enough in the thigh to drop him again. He shouts in pain and, as he goes down, I kick him in the ribs, allowing the rage to flow through me. This won't take as long as I'd hoped or planned, the anger is too consuming for me to play with this idiot. "You aren't where you're supposed to be."

He holds a hand out, a weak attempt to get me to pause my assault. I grin savagely. The moron just gave me something else to break. I take hold of his hand and break all five of his fingers in one swift move, crushing them in an punishing grip. He tries to pull his hand back to his chest in an attempt to cradle the injured appendage. I take hold of his arm and wrench it behind his back, bending until it breaks. I don't need him for anything. I've found my family. His death became a forgone conclusion the moment he betrayed the cartel, therefore there's no reason for me to pull my punches.

He screams in pain, his agony rending the evening, interrupting the haunting Cuban music that'd been playing in the background. I release his arm to hang limply by his side, step around the front of him and send my knee into his face. He's kind enough to hunch forward as I bring my knee up, increasing the impact. I've worked enough guys over in my life to know exactly what kind of damage I've done. His front teeth are now in the back of his throat and his navel cavity is caved in. I'm happy. His screams have become gurgles and I can hear the music again.

"Better," I say, sitting on the edge of his bed. I watch him try to crawl toward the door and laugh derisively. "You think you'll get far, Pedro?" I stand up and stride around to his front, taking in the hideous mask of his bloodied face. "No, hombre. There's no going forward, no going back… no going anywhere from this." I crouch next to him and place my hand on his shoulder, as if commiserating. "You took my wife and kids, Pedro. That's a death sentence by itself. But tonight, I watched as you put hands on my wife. I watched you touch what belongs to me, covet my woman."

He garbles something completely unintelligible, spitting out a streak of blood, saliva and teeth. Savage satisfaction rolls through me and I reach over him toward the tiny card table, picking up the pack of cigarettes and lighter. I light another one, blowing a stream of smoke down at Pedro.

"You know, I probably would've ended this quickly. Used a gun, put a bullet in your head while you slept." I allow an edge of regret to leak into my voice as I speak. "You were a good man. With the Zetas for a lot of years. Instead, you touched my Luna. Laid hands on her." Anger courses through me as I picture the way he pressed himself against her while she was forced to take his attentions. I'd stood in the back of the yard, hidden in the shadows, watching, taking in her reaction, making sure she wasn't encouraging him. The manner of her death would be determined by her actions since she fled Mexico. I yank his head back, pull the knife from my belt and slice his ear off. Gurgling screams erupt from his throat and blood gushes forth in a fountain. I release him so he doesn't get blood all over my jeans and shoes. I examine the blade, proud of the lethal edge I keep to my weapons. "Almost too bad I didn't let you keep your voice, would've been interesting to hear your weak justifications for taking another man's wife."

I sit back on the bed once more and watch him collapse on the floor in a pitiful heap, blood seeping from his head. His broken arm lays at an odd angle next to his body. I wipe the edge of my blade on his pillow and then tap it against my leg as I let him writhe in pain a little longer. I've found over the years that suffering is increased by two things; the expectation of more pain and the time it takes for the body to take stock of the damage done to it, for the pain receptors to go from blissful numbness to agonizing life as the body tries to recover.

His groans increase in volume as the fire of pain licks at him. I stand and circle him, wishing for a worthier opponent. A good fight might have released some pent-up frustration. Might have saved my wife from some of the seething hate running through my veins. Instead, he acts like nothing more than a slithering worm. Barely worthy of my notice, let alone the edge of my blade.

"You disgust me," I snarl, feeling suddenly tired. I drop my cigarette on the floor and crush it beneath my heel.

He cringes into the floor and rolls onto his back. He brings his hands up, one broken and mangled, and places them in a prayer position. He begs with his eyes. I grant his wish for death, slashing my knife in a downward arc through the material of his shirt, the soft tissue of his stomach and deep into the recesses of stomach cavity. He howls in pain while I slice through his bowels, making sure he will feel every moment of his death for the long hours to come.

The man that aided my wife's departure does not get to

die easily. He will go to hell wishing he'd made another choice. I pull my blade from his intestines as easily as if I sliced through butter. Another fist to the face and his screams turn to gurgles of agony. I stand, pleased that Pedro has learned his lesson.

I wipe my knife on his bed and sheath it once more. An image of Luna flashes through my mind and I fear that I will need it again soon enough. I'm unable to hold onto the thought of slicing her up, though I know there can be no other way. She's earned the justice that will be coming her way. As I leave the shack and make my way toward the house, I know it's eagerness to set eyes on her once more, touch her soft skin, hold her against me, sink inside her silken body that drives me forward.

There's no reason I can't fuck my wife before I release her from this mortal world. Perhaps she'll thank me. After Pedro's death I'm feeling benevolent, less vengeful. Maybe I'll be able to suppress the fury enough to send her on an orgasmic high before I kill her. She knows what must happen. Though purposefully oblivious on occasion, Luna is not a stupid woman.

I walk steadily toward the cottage a bleak calm settling over me. Soon I will see her again. The woman that I love, the woman I can never trust. She must be put down.

As I reach for the back door it flies open in my hand. I pull my gun and jump to the side, prepared to shoot the threat. When I see Alberto, I reholster my gun and straighten. "What the fuck, man?" I grumble and go to step around him.

He holds a hand out. "She's not here," he says grimly. "It looks like she took the children and ran as soon as we got here."

5

———

LUNA

I can't sleep.

I roll over onto my side and punch one of the extra pillows pulling it against my stomach. I think about going out to the kitchen for a shot or two of the Cuban rum I picked up in Havana today, but I fear that Pedro will see the light and think it is an invitation to come inside for a visit. I turn over again and sigh, staring at the faint light in the hall. I've been leaving the washroom light on with the door partially closed as a makeshift nightlight for the children. So far neither of them have needed to get up in the night. My little darlings have always been amazing sleepers, like their father. Unlike their mama.

I roll over again, turning my back to the hallway, and hug the pillow tight against me. I close my eyes. Andres immediately fills my mind, his dark, tattooed body stalking to the forefront. I bury my face into the bedding and release a muffled sob. There's no help for it. I can't stop thinking of him. I never could. He's been the only man for me since the moment I set eyes on him five years ago.

I was nineteen.

I lived at home still, with my mama, Julia. She was the prettiest, most sought after woman in our small Mexican town. She never said she made a mistake with my papá, because she loved me too much to tell me I wasn't wanted. But I knew. I'm not stupid. I stayed home to help mama pay rent. It was hard to find jobs in our territory, especially for women. Most jobs were paid for on their backs. My mama... she wasn't having any of that shit. She was a hard worker, even though a woman with her looks didn't have to work.

I, on the other hand, took advantage of the many offers that started coming my way when I turned 14 and my curves filled in. I didn't fuck around with them... for the most part. Mama would've killed them and then me if she thought I was selling my body for money. No, I just used men, dangled them on my little finger and greased them for as much as I could get. I learned the art of flirtation at an early age and used it for as much as I could possibly get for me and my family. Once I'd assured mama that I wasn't prostituting myself, she seemed happy to partake of the money, jewelry and other gifts that were showered on me.

I met Andres at a bar just outside Los Zetas territory. It was near the small town I lived in. My friend, Sonja, convinced me I would find richer, better looking prey if I widened my hunting grounds. She wasn't entirely wrong. I'd exhausted the pool of willing saps in the town where I lived and, since I wasn't willing to commit, I needed to find a new haunt. The evening I met my future husband I wore the sluttiest jeans I owned, a pair of ripped up skinny jeans that may as well have been glued to my ass and hips. I topped it with a black half corset, fire engine red lipstick and my favourite pair of lucky cowgirl boots that I'd bought in Tijuana.

When we arrived, it was to discover that we weren't the

only ones with this brilliant plan. One of the resident whores from my small town, a bitch that actually sold herself, was perched on a barstool, talking shit about me and mine. Marta Sanchez. I'd known her since grade school, long enough for the two of us to develop a decent hatred of each other. Well, I couldn't have this smack-talking whore bad-mouthing my mama in some other town. Especially not behind my back. Nope. She was going to do that shit right in front of me where I could cut her up for daring.

"Please don't," Sonja whispered, clutching my arm. "I think there's some cartel guys in here."

"You might want to stand away from the blood spray," I muttered back, peeling her fingers away and stalking toward the bar, my eyes narrowing on Marta.

"Well fuck me, if it isn't my home town whore!" Marta shouted when I got close enough for her to spot me. Her shrill voice carried throughout the bar. "Her mama used to be pretty and now this one thinks she's hot shit."

"Keep talking, bitch!" I snarled as I approached.

She must've drank too much for self-preservation to kick in because she remained seated, a cruel smile twisting her bright-pink painted lips while everyone within her vicinity scattered.

"You think you're so fucking hot," she said, pointing at me. "You're nothing but a pair of tits and a bad fuck when the guys can't find someone better. Go back home, Luna. No one wants you in these parts. You ain't got nothing they want. Go take care of your broken-down whore of a mama."

I didn't respond verbally. I grabbed a fistful of her curly hair and dragged her off the bar stool. Her back hit the floor so hard the empty chairs around us rattled. I reached for a beer bottle brought it down hard against the side of bar, smashing it. I'd never really been in a true bar fight before but at that moment I was pretty happy I'd practiced smashing empties out behind my house.

I leapt on top of Marta, grabbed her by the hair and smashed her head into the floor, dazing her. When her eyes started to focus once more I brought the jagged edge of the bottle to her throat and snarled, "You will apologize about my mama. Right. Fucking. Now."

She turned her head to the side and spat then looked up and gave me a bloody half grin. "Make me, puta. You're just like her, making your money on your back."

I saw red. I didn't care that I'd never really been in a fight in my life, didn't care that there were all kinds of witnesses, I was going to cut this bitch. Make her regret her own birth. I lifted my arm, about to bring my hand down in a dramatic swing and cut her face open. Take out at least one of my competition. But before I could cut the bitch, my wrist was seized from behind in a strong, uncompromising grip. I frowned and glanced back over my shoulder. I met the bluest, sexiest most alluring eyes I'd ever seen on a Mexican man.

I recognized him instantly from his tattoos, his massive build and his arrogant attitude. Los Zetas. He was cartel. Holy. Shit. Despite the death I read in his eyes, I could feel myself instantly respond to him; my heart beat faster, my cheeks flushed and my body started to melt right then and there.

"You sure you want to do that, chica?" he asked, his deep voice filtering through my angry haze, turning my nipples diamond hard.

My gaze rolled back toward my victim still laying frozen beneath me, her eyes squeezed shut now. She seemed to have figured out that I meant business with the broken end of a beer bottle. I studied her for a moment, trying to feel sympathy for the psycho whore cunt that had called my mama names in front of an entire bar. Nope, nothing.

I nodded my head. "Yes, definitely," I said earnestly batting my lashes at him and giving him the big deep brown, almost black eyes that usually worked on all of my male prey. He seemed completely unmoved.

"Have you ever cut anyone before?" he asked idly, his thumb caressing the sensitive spot on the back of my wrist underneath my thumb.

I shook my head. "No, but Marta seems like a good start." Her eyes were starting to open and I saw hope reflected there. I glared death at her, assuring her with my own eyes that she better start melting back into the floor because as soon as this hombre dropped my hand she was DONE.

He nodded and continued to caress my skin, his thumb making circling motions. "The feel of flesh under a blade is not something you should take lightly, Luna. I know this well. You cut her up, and it will stay with you for life." His deep voice caressing my name, his words, the emotion he allowed me to see in those gorgeous, bottomless eyes, they pierced me.

I nodded my head thoughtfully. I believed him. This was a man that had seen darkness and death. Had lived it and something in him didn't want me to see the same things. I dropped the bottle. He grinned at me, showing me a dimple in his cheek. I realized he must be younger than I thought; maybe twenty or twenty-one.

"Th-thank you," Marta said gratefully from underneath me.

My head snapped down and I drew my fist back, sending it flying into her face. The back of her head hit the floor hard with a satisfying thump. I grinned and looked up at the incredibly gorgeous Los Zetas crouched over top of me. He offered me his hand and I took it, allowing him to help me up.

"Let's go, sweet Luna."

I went with him and we spent the rest of the night making love, exploring each other and indulging in a sensual tasting unlike anything I'd ever done before. When we finally sated our desires for a few hours at a time, we talked. Andres wanted to know everything about me, even though it wasn't an exciting story. He asked endless questions, frowning fiercely if I dared to mention other men. At one point, when I told him the truth about my reason for being in the bar he apparently frequented, he'd become so annoyed, he'd flipped me right over and fucked me from behind, demanding that I never again do anything so reckless.

One night turned into a day, and a day turned into a weekend. At the end of that weekend I'd insisted that I needed to go see my mama, explain why I wasn't home. Even though I was a flirt, I wasn't a loose kind of woman. I didn't usually stay away for entire nights. I was shocked when Andres refused to allow me to leave. Even he seemed confused by his own possessive anger over my need to go home. Finally, he agreed that it was ridiculous to keep me locked away from my family and friends.

I made the promise that I would come back and he allowed me to leave. Our separation didn't last longer than a few hours. I'd barely walked through my front door, said hello to my mama and tried to explain my absence when the big Mexican conqueror came striding in behind me, uncaring that he hadn't been invited in.

I sigh and smile into my pillow as I picture the confrontation between him and mama. She'd made only one protest and then he'd swept her away by both dogged determination and charm, assuring her that his intentions were honourable; that he wanted to marry me the moment we could find a church. A warm rush of feeling had swept over me as I'd listened to him speak to my only living relative. Logical arguments had popped up in my brain, but each time I tried to fight with myself, my gaze was drawn back to him. I couldn't believe my luck. Couldn't believe a man like this wanted a girl like me.

I came from nothing, living like a pauper, on my wits and will alone. It amazed me that a man as good looking and connected as Andres could possibly want me for more than a good night's fuck. And I'd done exactly what I'd sworn never to do, given up the goods at the blink of an eye. I thought I would come back home to my small town with my small, lonely life and stay here until I died. I never thought I'd see the powerful, sexy mobster again. Perhaps a small part of me was relieved at the prospect, knew I was safer, saner, if I walked away and didn't look back. That life wasn't for a small-town girl like me.

But then he showed up at my door. Spoke like a man in love. He even convinced mama. Or at least convinced her that he planned on kidnapping me, dragging me to the alter and eventually impregnating me, and there was nothing she could do to stop him; that if she wanted a relationship with her daughter and future grandbabies then she'd better sanction the union.

We were married the next day with only my mother and one of his brothers to stand up with us. It was such a whirlwind. Before I knew what was happening, I was on a plane to Paris for a new wardrobe and then Cuba for the rest of our honeymoon. It was terrifying, it was exciting, it was the happiest time in my life. Because I had never seen my husband more relaxed and carefree than those two weeks that we'd taken away from real life, away from the Los Zetas.

Once we returned to The Site and Andres returned to his life within the organization, our marriage became a terrifying struggle between his brutal dark side and my ability to ignore everything that went on around me. Before I could question myself, question my values and the horrors I knew I shouldn't keep turning away from, I became pregnant. A terrifying and exhilarating prospect. My baby, my Cristo, gave me something else to focus on. Gave Andres and me someone else to love.

But then Andres started disappearing, coming home less frequently and when he did, the black aura of death would cling to him and I'd know he'd been on a particularly brutal job. I would beg him to come home. But he would still disappear, sometimes for weeks at a time, sometimes longer. Once he didn't come home for over two months. When he did finally show up on our doorstep he was a burnt-out shadow of his former self. And though he promised me he would never do it again, I knew drug addicts. Had grown up around them in my small town. Heard stories from mama about my deadbeat daddy. Once an addict, always an addict. Eventually the pull of the drug would be too much for him. More than his love for his family. I'd had no choice but to ask Charlie to step in. Since that terrible time I know that Andres has controlled his habit. I used it against him, throwing it in his face as my reason for leaving. I lied to him.

I sit up in bed with a sigh and shove hair out of my face. I know I won't be able to sleep. I decide to try to find the rum without turning any lights on. I need a couple of shots before I can settle down. I slide off the bed and reach for my robe, tying it loosely around my middle. I pad barefoot down the hall, past the washroom, around the corner toward the kitchen, squinting in the darkness. Very little light filters through the windows here. We're too far on the outskirts of Havana to see city lights.

I turn the corner and reach for the cupboard. My fingers just barely graze the handle when I'm seized from behind, lifted right of the floor and slammed into a hard chest, a hand covering my mouth. Panic engulfs my mind and I kick out, striking the fridge with the heel of my foot. I think Andres must have me and has covered my mouth so we won't wake the children, but I realize quickly I'm wrong. The man holding me doesn't feel like my husband, doesn't smell like my husband.

It doesn't take me long to realize that whoever is holding me doesn't want to hurt me. I stop panicking and let myself go limp, gripping his arm. He gentles his hold and starts whispering rapidly in my ear.

"We don't have much time," he says. "Soon as Andres is done playing with Pedro, he'll be in here looking for you."

A chill slithers through my heart as I realize who has me. Alberto. Andres' best friend and second-in-command. I begin shaking in his arms. I don't understand why he isn't immediately turning me over to my husband. Why he's saying this to me. As though he intends to help me. I try to speak, but my words are muffled by his hand. He has more to say and he wants to get it out quickly before we're interrupted.

"You must take the children and go, run far away from here, Luna," he says against my ear. The scent of his cologne wafts between us and I know that smell will forever be burned into my memory along with the confusion and terror of this moment. I despise Alberto's touch, but he's giving me a chance so I settle and listen. "Andres intends to kill you, and I can't let that happen. When I release you, you will run. Comprende?"

I nod frantically, my lips pressing hard against his fingers. He releases me and shoves me away from him. I stumble forward and catch myself against the edge of the fridge. I take three running steps toward the hall without looking back, instinct guiding me to my children. Then I wheel around, my hands on either wall and squint at him in the darkness.

"Why, Alberto?" I ask, my voice harsh and dry from terror.

He doesn't answer at first. He stalks forward, grips my arms and drags me down the hall, shoving me toward Cristo's room, pointing with a demanding finger. I nod and reach for the knob. His hand lands on mine and he stops me. I look up, fear shuddering through me, positive he must have changed his mind.

"I love him like a brother," he grunts, his voice low. "Your death will destroy him. If you die by his hand, he won't survive. I debated taking you out myself to save him the trouble. If there were no kids, it's what would've happened tonight."

I lift my hand to crush the sob that escapes my throat. I've known Alberto as long as I've known Andres. I have tried my best to love and respect this man, but I also know that I've never earned his respect in return. He's been suspicious of me and my motives from the beginning. He knows as well as I that I never fit in with the Los Zetas.

"Go," he says, releasing my hand and stepping back into the shadows.

6

ANDRES

Two days.

It takes two extra days, a truly impressive amount of resources and some deadly persuasion to find my wife and children. Forty-eight more hours should have given me plenty of extra time to calm down, to approach the imminent apprehension of my wife with less emotion. Instead, I'm angrier, more blazingly furious than I had been when I first set out to find her.

I have lost my best friend. Alberto's betrayal is sharp, like the invisible blade that cuts deep from under the ribcage. It hadn't taken me long to realize that there was only one way for my helpless, unskilled wife to figure out I was in the vicinity, to run into the night with our children, only her purse and the clothes on her back.

We'd shed tears together, Alberto and I, when I finally got the truth out of him. And though he didn't deserve it, I let him have a dignified death. One bullet to the temple for his betrayal. He'd seen it coming, hadn't even put up a fight. Gave me his reasons for letting the bitch go and stood still as a statue while I sent him to his death.

Now I'm finally closing in on her, the woman who caused all of this. Hatred burns hot and black in my heart. The heart that once beat only for her, my Luna, my everything. No longer. Now she is nothing. She is ashes.

I watch as her boat takes a reckless turn, tipping to the side against a particularly large wave in its attempt to avoid us. We're so close behind them that I can hear her voice cry out sharp in the night. I know that she is terrified for the children, urging the man who is commanding the small speedboat to slow down, to not take the waves with such speed lest he overturns the boat. Neither of my children can swim.

Fury, my constant companion these past several days, surges as my boat, a much more powerful prospect than the one Luna is on, pulls up alongside. I can see the captain of her vessel, a weather-beaten Cuban man, glancing over his shoulder, fear etched into his wrinkles. He should be afraid. There will be no mercy for the man helping my family, the man disregarding my children's lives.

I pull my gun, take aim and shoot the captain in the leg. He immediately goes down on one leg. The boat swerves to the side and mine is forced to compensate, slowing down so they don't crash. As soon as the captain straightens out, I command my vessel to pull up alongside again. Once we're even I shout, "Stop, or the next bullet finds your skull!"

Most of my words are lost to the wind, but my tone of voice and the lift of my weapon is threat enough. He pushes forward on the throttle, slowing the boat. As ours slows too, I finally do what I've been avoiding, I glance toward the back of the boat. The sight that greets me crushes a heart that I've thought grown cold and hard by Luna's betrayal. She is sitting on the bottom of the boat, sobbing, her arms wrapped around each of our children.

My chest begins heaving in anger. I'm absolutely furious at the man captaining the small vessel for recklessly disregarding the safety of my small family. I am terribly, brutally angry with Luna that she has brought us to this moment. I'm so fucking mad that I feel anything for her at all, that I'm concerned for her well-being. That she might have been hurt during her dash for the border. Fuck, it hurts me that her narrow shoulders are shaking and that she refuses to look up at me.

Cristo is shouting at me, his arms wrapped firmly around Luna's neck, but I can't hear what he's saying. Sola is cradled safely in Luna's lap, a life jacket secured around her tiny body. I can tell that she's crying too, probably because her mama is hysterical, and she doesn't know what to do.

"What do you want us to do with them, my friend?" A deep voice asks from beside me.

I glanced toward my Cuban contact, an ex-American marine that moved to Cuba decades ago and runs arms through several countries in the region. I didn't tell him much about my reason for being in Cuba, just gave him a brief description of Luna and the children, told him where I thought they might go. I knew she was too smart to take one of the few airports as an out, which left the docks. Sure enough, she was caught trying to make a run for Miami. Though obvious, it was her best bet. A short piece of water, a quick boat ride in the middle of the night. She'd obviously greased a few palms that weren't connected to someone who would turn her in.

Unfortunately for her, courtesy of my American friend, I had men crawling all over the docks in Havana, Varadaro and any surrounding port. She is well and truly fucked.

"Take the children, keep them safe. Someone will come

for them, take them back to Mexico," I finally tell him. "I will deal with my wife."

Their boat slows to a crawl and finally stops. I grin as the captain falls backwards on his ass, his bloodied leg straight out in front of him. He clutches his thigh right above the gunshot wound. I step up onto the edge of our boat and over onto his. I can sense the moment Luna lifts her head and looks at me, can feel the heat of her eyes on my back.

I stride toward the captain and lift my gun. He starts to protest but I put a bullet through his head. He collapses to the deck in a heap. I can hear Luna crying behind me, trying to calm the children. Seconds later her sharp screams rend the air. I turn slowly, hardening myself, knowing what I'll see.

Alex and his men are separating Luna from the children. For a brief moment I question myself, question if I should step forward to comfort my children, tell them that they will be safe, taken care of. But I shake this weakness away. They have spent years coddled by a mother that has refused to understand her place. Now her punishment will be death. I was raised within the Los Zetas organization and I will die there, as will my children. It is time they learn their place. I watch dispassionately as they're removed from their mother.

Luna screams and lunges after the men taking her children away. One of Alex's men knocks her back. She rocks back on the boat, already unstable from the choppy waves and falls, hitting the bench behind her so hard it knocks the wind from her. Fury rises, and I want to murder the man that dared to touch my wife. Instead I reach for her, taking her arm in a hard grip as she tries to push herself up, guided now by desperate maternal instinct. She cares now about nothing else other than going after her children and taking them away from the strangers. She doesn't seem to care that she is smaller and outnumbered.

"Luna," I growl, swinging her around to face me.

I can tell by her unfocused eyes and pale cheeks that she doesn't hear or see me anymore. So I hold her tight in my arms and nod at the Alex, telling him without words that the other boat can leave.

"Cristo," I shout, finally acknowledging my son. His head snaps up from where he's crouched on the other boat, comforting his sobbing sister. "Take care of Sola. I'll see you soon."

"What about mama?" he yells back.

I study my son as the other boat begins to pull away. He's only four, but he's intelligent. He probably knew the moment Luna fled with them in the middle of the night that she was doing something she wasn't supposed to. That there would be consequences. I nod grimly at my son and turn away without answering.

7

LUNA

His scent fills my mind, teasing my senses, and sending me into a spiral of confusion. Andres usually represents safety, love, strength and so much more. I know he's here to murder me, to torture and hurt me, but my body wants to sink into him, to cling to his hard body and beg him to hold me. Andres is like coming home. There's just something about him that I recognize on a deep, subconscious level.

Once the other boat pulls away he lets go of me as though he can't stand to touch me. I sink to the deck, my shaky legs unable to hold my weight up. I crawl to the other side and watch as the boat holding my children grows distant, tears pouring down my cheeks. I don't bother to check them. There's no point. This is probably the last time I'll see Cristo and Sola; my heart is breaking.

I hear a splash and look over. The body of the captain is gone. I assume Andres has just thrown him into the ocean. I shudder, imagining it could have just as easily been me, except Andres will want to keep me alive a little longer so we can discuss my error in leaving him and my extreme colossal mistake in taking his children. A sob escapes and I drop my head into my arms against the bench. There's not much else I can do at this point.

I feel the engine shudder to life and nearly fall backwards as the boat leaps forward. I cling to the seat, still sitting on the floor of the boat. I finally wipe my tears against my sleeve and peek up at Andres where he stands at the helm. His back is to me. He can't seem to look at me. Or perhaps he can't be bothered. I know when it comes to Los Zetas, if a person betrays, they become less than nothing, and this is not my first betrayal. The first was quickly swept aside. This one won't be.

His refusal to look at me can be my one chance at survival if I'm brave enough to take it. I can jump off the boat and make a run for the United States. I will lose my children. A thought that makes me want to die, but I am stronger than that. Perhaps one day I will find a way to be with them again. They will remember this day, remember the father that separated them from their mama.

I am halfway to Miami and I'm a strong swimmer. One of the few skills I've managed to hone over the years. I try not to think of shark infested waters and edge toward the back of the boat, gripping the seat cushions in my shaking hands. If Andres suspects, he'll try to stop me and I know that I'd rather die in an escape attempt than under his hands. As I reach the back, I pull myself up, reaching for the railing along the side.

I stand up on the seat and wobble a little as the boat hits a wave. I glance at Andres, who is concentrating on his destination, the distant, brightly lit shores of Miami. I look away, step up to the railing and dive over the side. Cool, dark water instantly engulfs me, enveloping my entire body and head. I close my eyes and allow myself to sink a few metres, before bringing my arms up and pulling myself toward the surface. The first thing I do is listen for the boat and pray that he hasn't turned it around. As soon as my head breaks the surface I open my eyes and start looking around.

I can't see the boat. Even worse. I can't hear it. I blink water out of my eyes, shove my dark hair back and twist and turn until I'm oriented to the far-off twinkling lights. Then I start swimming for my life. I barely make it several strokes when strong arms snatch me back against a hard chest. I open my mouth to scream but a wave hits us and my mouth fills with salty ocean water.

"You stupid bitch," he snarls as soon as we're able to surface again. "Are you trying to kill yourself?"

He clamps an arm around my neck and hauls me quickly through the water in hard fast strokes. I can't see where he's going until he hits something. I realize it's the side of the boat. He reaches up and pulls a small ladder down, then using his enormous strength, yanks me out of water with him. I fight to remain standing when we step onto the deck, but he shoves me against the bench. I fall, landing on my hip. I bite my lip to keep from crying out. He searches the boat and comes up with rope. I flinch away as he stalks back toward me. He brings my hands forward and ties them together.

When he's finished, he grips my chin and forces my face up. I think he's about to say something, but he doesn't. He just stares down at me, studying my face in the moonlight. I stare back at him, caressing his chiselled features with my gaze. His olive-toned skin, his wet, black hair, the tattoo peeking out of the top of his wet T-shirt. His stubble is coming in, as though he hasn't shaved since I left. I want to run my fingers along his jaw, feel the texture against my skin. I can feel my body warming in response to him, preparing for my husband.

I lower my eyes, letting my eyelashes drift down. He finally releases my chin and turns away. He starts the boat again and pulls the throttle, turning towards Miami. A chill slithers down my spine, chasing away my previous heat. Why is he taking us the States?

I huddle in the bottom of the boat, dropping my head onto my knees, the wet strands of my hair falling around me. I can't remember the last time I've felt this miserable. From the moment we met I've been Andres' pampered, petted princess. The light and love of his life. Now I resemble a drowned cat. My hair is such a tangled mess I'm not sure it will ever recover and several of my fingernails are chipped and broken. I sneak one into my mouth to nibble on the edge in an attempt to smooth it, the move awkward since my wrists are tied together.

Then I realize what I'm doing, worrying over my appearance. Typical Luna. When faced with enormous adversity, I turn to what I know, vanity. I laugh bitterly, the sound lost in the rushing wind as we speed rapidly toward our destination. In the space of less than a week my life has changed entirely. I have gone from my beautiful, perfect mansion, my jewels, designer clothes and celebrity make up brands to becoming a dead woman walking.

"Stand up," Andres growls at me, loud enough that I can hear his voice over the engine and elements.

I lift my head to look at him. He's staring down at me, his sharp features harder than ever, utterly inscrutable. There isn't a single ounce of forgiveness there. For one wild second I frantically consider killing myself. I know it will be faster than whatever he is planning for me. But my husband is smarter and faster than that. He'll get to me before I can do anything to myself and I know I'm too weak-willed to truly hurt myself.

I grip the back of the seat and pull myself up, struggling to stand on limbs shaking with fatigue. I cling to the back of the passenger chair and turn my head, staring out toward the city of Miami, brightly lighting the sky. I squint as the wind stings my eyes and cheeks and I bring my bound hands up to protect my face. I wonder where Andres plans to take us. I had been assured by my contact in Cuba that there would be someone on the beach to meet me and the children.

My question is soon answered as he steers our tiny boat right into one of Miami's huge dockyards. I hold my breath, awe and trepidation filling my heart. Massive container ships surround us on both sides. I want to cling to my husband as we weave between these huge beasts that could so easily crush us, but I know he will provide no comfort.

He pulls the boat up to a smaller dock, one that is meant for boats like ours. He cuts the engine and quickly ties it off. Then he leaps onto the dock and turns to glare down at me.

"Come," he snaps.

I flinch and ease back against the seat I'm clinging too. I know my hesitation is pointless, but I can't seem to bring myself to walk willingly toward certain doom. He growls impatiently, steps back onto the boat, rocking it wildly and grips my bound wrists. He turns and hauls us both out onto the huge dock. I bite my lip again to keep from crying out as my wrists chafe against the rope. I've been doing that a lot, holding in my sounds of pain. I know soon those moans will turn to screams.

We walk side by side across the dock, eerily lit up by huge yellow lights. I stumble in an attempt to keep up with Andres' long strides and wince as I stub my toe. The ballet flats I'd chosen to wear had been lost when I jumped in the water. My feet are now bare and my dark blue hooded sweatshirt and thin white trousers are thoroughly soaked.

Andres is just as wet, but he seems uncaring or unaware of any discomfort. He's wearing his usual working outfit of thick, black combat trousers and a black T-shirt, stretched taut over his muscular chest. The only thing that's missing is his vest with the red Z for Los Zetas. I wonder if he's bothered to change at all since he started hunting for his family. Sadness over what I've done to him begins to eat away at me. Perhaps I should have tried talking to him again, just one more time. Maybe told him the truth about why I left.

But I know my Andres, he won't listen. He never listens. He loves his family, but his loyalty is elsewhere. It's been trained into him since birth.

I nearly jump out of my skin when a man materializes out of the darkness, striding swiftly to meet us. I cower against Andres, who tightens his hold on my hand. I'm not sure anymore if this is a protective gesture or his way of keeping me from escaping. I don't care. I take comfort in his firm hold.

"Decena," the man grunts.

I see something glowing in his hand and stare curiously until I realize it's a cigar. He lifts it to his lips and takes a long, deep draw before exhaling the pungent smoke. Andres nods, but doesn't say anything.

"You got something there, friend?" he asks, a leer in his harsh voice. I shudder and press myself tighter against Andres. "Didn't know you'd be travelling with a package. Pretty little thing, isn't she?"

I feel tension vibrate through Andres, rippling the muscles of the arm that I cling to. I squeeze my eyes shut hoping that this won't end in the same way as my boat's captain. Andres seems even more trigger happy than usual, as though his emotions are a hairbreadth away from exploding into white hot fury, taking down everyone within range.

Andres ignores the man's musing and says, "You have the items I requested?"

The guy is quiet for a moment and then he says, "The car is just inside the gates, passports and money in the glovebox. I'll let you out once the funds are in my account."

"Check," Andres grunts, striding past, his hand on my bound wrists, dragging me with him. "The money is already there."

The other guy attempts to keep up, tries to say something else, but Andres acts as though he doesn't exist. My heart pounds in agitation. This is not my Andres, not my sweet, carefree husband, quick to laugh and chat with the guys. This man who is holding on to me is a man that I fear. The man that I fled, because more and more I have seen his darkness surface. This is the man our son will become if he stays in the cartel.

This last thought brings the fear and pain rushing back to the surface as I remember the way my children were torn from me. As we walk I desperately want to ask Andres what will happen to our babies, but I don't dare speak to him. I have to comfort myself with the thought that Andres loves them as much as I do, he won't allow anything bad to happen to them.

We quickly find the car as it's the only one sitting under a streetlight in a mostly empty parking lot just inside the dockyard. I gasp and trip, falling forward as a rock bites viciously into the heel of my foot. Without breaking stride Andres grips my arm and swings me easily up into his arms. I sink gratefully into the heat of his chest and press my face against his neck. I know I shouldn't, know that I should hold myself stiff. But my exhausted body and brain can do nothing but recognize the basic comfort of my husband.

He opens the passenger door of the car and drops me inside, nearly flinging me away from him. I grip the console and swing my knees to the side so I won't get caught with the door when he slams it shut. He gets in the other side, pulls a set of keys from beneath his seat and starts the car. It's an older model sedan, definitely not something we would normally drive.

I flinch back in my seat as he reaches toward me, but he only pops the glovebox open. He pulls an envelope out and checks the contents. Without saying a word he tosses the envelope on the back seat and slams the glovebox closed again. Then he reaches around me and drags my seatbelt across my body. I lift my arms automatically so they won't get caught as he latches it.

The moment the dockyard gates begin to open he hits the gas, driving quickly away from the ships and the creepy man that provided our getaway.

Unable to hold back any longer I peek at him and ask timidly, "Where are we going, Andres?"

He doesn't answer for a moment and I think maybe he won't respond. He doesn't have to. I'm at his mercy, I'll go with him wherever he chooses to take me. Finally, he turns his head to look at me, pinning me with those intense blue eyes. "I'm taking you where no one will think to look," he says grimly. "Where no one will find you, Luna."

8

ANDRES

She has finally fallen asleep. A combination of terror and sheer physical exhaustion overwhelming her. I stand over her, staring down, frustrated. Despite her bedraggled appearance, she is just as beautiful as the day we met. Perhaps, more so for being the mother of my children. I try to call on the hatred that is required for the coming days, but it's tempered and twisted with the obsessive love that has been my constant companion from the moment I set eyes on this woman.

Luna was a glorious sight to behold, that first time I set eyes on her. I feel like I've spent a lifetime replaying it in my head, the impact was so intense. She must've been in the bar for at least a few minutes before I noticed her, but I hadn't seen her walk in. When the disturbance began I didn't even bother to look. Hell, a bar like that, in that territory on a Friday night... fights weren't unusual. Then the guy next to me dropped his jaw and spat out his beer. This guy was a hardened criminal from my own squad. His reaction made it worth a look.

Seeing Luna take that woman off a bar stool and

straddle her on that dirty wooden floor was going to feature in my fantasies for years to come. She was a she-devil, screaming at the other woman about her mama. Then, when she lifted that broken bottle, I fell in love. A woman that looked like that, willing to cut the shit out of her adversary for daring to insult someone she loved had to belong to me. I wanted every ounce of her loyalty along with that curvy little package. So I intervened, took her out of that bar and back to my place. We've been inseparable ever since. Up until five days ago, when she left me without a word.

She shivers in her sleep, curling tighter on her side, seeking warmth in the airy cushion of the luxury leather jetliner seat. I fight the instinct to find a blanket and cover her slight form, provide for her needs as I have these past five years. Instead I remain standing, impassive, a guard in the night.

I've borrowed this private jet from a contact. Someone friendly with the Mexican Los Zetas. I know that word will get back to my brothers of this unexpected trip. I was forced to lie to my friend, tell him that I was taking my wife on a second honeymoon overseas and that we wanted to keep it quiet from potential enemies. I know there are holes in my story. Why didn't we take our own jet? Why last minute in the middle of the night? I will deal with the fallout later, after I've dealt with Luna.

For now, I'm satisfied that my children are safely on their way back to Mexico and my wife is at my mercy. I glance down at her and reach out to touch her face, helpless against the pull of her intoxicating allure. Her skin feels fragile and soft beneath my callused fingertips. She has always been this way for me. Almost worse than the heroin I spent years slamming into my veins. Luna is the drug that rapes my soul. The drug that I knew would one day shred my heart and everything else she's sunk her claws into.

I was right.

She ran away. Without explanation. Without thought or apology, she turned tail, stole my whole world and ran into the night. I clench my fist over her slumbering body, shaking with the need to destroy her, to end her here and now. My heart is thundering with the conflict. I vow that before she dies, I will strip her bare, flay the skin from her body and hear her scream her reasons for leaving. I will take satisfaction from her as she bleeds before me, begging on her knees, and then, perhaps, I will allow her to die.

My hand falls and I turn away, dropping into the seat next to her. I reach across, pick up a discarded blanket and throw it over her.

9

LUNA

We land just as morning begins to light the sky, splashing colours of orange and red across the clouds while we descend. I lean as much as I dare in my seat, trying to see where we are. I woke up several minutes ago, completely disoriented, without a clue as to how long we've been flying. I know I can't ask Andres where our destination is. One glance at him tells me he has sunk into a deep, angry silence. I'm not willing to draw his attention back to me. Not yet.

There's too much cloud cover for me to see where we are. The plane lands with a bounce and swiftly taxis to a stop. Before I have a chance to move, Andres unbuckles my seatbelt and pulls me out of my chair. I lurch to my feet and follow him to the door, smothering a yawn.

A flight attendant stands beside the airplane door, awaiting the pilot's go ahead to open it. She glances at me, disdain bright in her pretty blue eyes as she sweeps a glance over me from head to toe, stopping on my bare feet. I narrow my eyes, giving her my haughtiest stare, honed from years of spending money in the most expensive shops around the world.

"I heard the shopping was so good here," I murmur, casting a sly glance at Andres, "that I thought I would replace my entire wardrobe."

Her expression turns to confusion and she opens her mouth to speak, but Andres interrupts her, reaching back to squeeze my arm, his grip so tight that my eyes water in pain. "Forgive my wife. She's simply fishing for our destination. I'm taking her on a surprise honeymoon, but she can't stand the suspense."

The flight attendant flashes him a mega-watt smile that makes me want to claw the eyeballs right out of her face. "Well isn't that just so sweet of y'all," she simpers, sugar dripping from every word. "I hope you enjoy yourselves. The weather is supposed to be fantastic!"

"Thank you," Andres says and gestures toward the door impatiently.

Her smile droops a little. I don't blame her for trying. Andres is a beautiful man. His tattoos and broad muscular shoulders give him a dark, somewhat sinister air, but his youthful visage, coupled with his boyish charm draws women like flies to honey. Unfortunately, most women don't know his dark side. I don't really know his dark side. Not yet.

She opens the door and I'm greeted by the sharp, heady scent of ocean. Before my feet can touch the tarmac, I'm swung up into Andres arms once more. I reach automatically for his neck, holding tight as we make our way rapidly across an empty airfield toward an object. I squint and cover my eyes against the glare of the sun. I realize that this is another conveniently placed car for our benefit. The Decena reach seems never-ending.

Fatigue hits me all over again as we drive, and though I

know I should pay close attention to wherever we're driving in case I'm somehow able to escape, I'm barely able to keep my eyes open. As the warmth of the sun penetrates my window, caressing my hair and skin, I lean heavily against the door and I feel myself begin to drift.

I'm not sure how long we drive or if I sleep, but I find myself being shaken awake, Andres' blue eyes blazing down at me. "Get out," he snaps. Before I'm even fully aware he's gone, his door slams behind him. The car rocks with the force of his departure.

My heart thumps in trepidation as I gingerly open my own door and pull myself out, using the doorframe for balance. I'm weary with fatigue, my body feels sore and I'm terrified of what's to come. I glance around. My jaw drops and I stare in numb fascination at the scene in front of me. It's so breathtaking that for a moment I forget who I'm with and why we're here. A wide, sparkling sea stretches out in front of me, the morning sun turning the peaks of each wave into jewels.

I step away from the car to get a better look and realize that I'm standing almost at the edge of a cliff. The cliff is surrounded by scrub bushes and grass. A look down shows me a narrow sandy beach far below being pounded by crashing waves. I don't see anyone and assume it must be private or difficult to access. I turn slowly on the spot and look behind me. Andres is watching me intently as I realize exactly how isolated we are. There is a house behind him. It's small and utilitarian. I look in every direction but realize there are no other buildings in the area. We're completely alone.

No one will hear me scream.

"Come," he says and turns toward the house, turning his back on me, expecting that I will follow.

I have no other choice. The car keys are in his pocket and I couldn't possibly get them away from him. Even if I somehow manage to get in the car and drive away without him catching me, where would I go? I don't know where we are. Andres has ensured I'm completely helpless.

I trail after him, into the cabin-like house. He closes the door behind me and attempts to turn a light on, but nothing happens. I see him frown through the sunlight filtering through the dusty window. He seems to shrug off the minor problem and crouches by a cupboard, digging around. He pulls out several candles and a flashlight, setting them on top. It quickly becomes clear to me that he's been here before. Somehow the reality of my situation hits home in that moment, driving away my numbness. Andres has brought me to a remote location, someplace he's been but I never have. A place that he likely intends to leave alone. A place that I will never leave.

I try to stifle a sob but fail. I know he won't want me to ask questions, that he only wants answers, but I have to know. "A-Andres... please tell me where our babies are." My voice breaks as I force the words out. "Please? I need to know."

His head snaps up and his crystal-like blue eyes pin me to the spot. He ignores my question and I know he won't tell me where Sola and Cristo are. Finally, he speaks, rising slowly from the floor. "We have some things to talk about, you and I."

Standing he towers over me by almost a foot. His height and gorgeous hard, muscular body have always attracted me. Now these things terrify me. They highlight how much weaker I am than him. I back up until I hit the wall. I place the palms of my hands against the wood, trying to centre myself.

"Yes, Andres," I whisper. "L-let's talk."

He stalks forward and slams his palm into the wall next to my head. The entire wall shakes and I flinch to the side. He grabs me and hauls me back up, holding me between his arms. He stares down at me, showing me the true extent of his rage. I read death in his expression. Not because there is an expression on his face, but because there is none. There is nothing on my beloved's face. He is blank.

My heart shatters. But I feel stronger. Maybe I will die by his hands. Maybe it'll be a horrible death, but I know, looking into the death mask that is Andres' face, that I made the right decision. I tried to take my children away from this life. I tried to give my son another life, another option besides the constant death that has twisted his father.

"Talk," he says, his voice low and deadly. "Say your piece, Luna. This is the only chance you will get."

I lick my lips and nod. Yes, I will tell him. He deserves that much from me. But first, I deserve something from him. For five years of marriage, of love and loyalty. I deserve to know my fate. "I will tell you, Andres," I whisper, my voice shaking under the onslaught of his fury. "But first, I want to know what you intend to do to me."

He laughs, the sound harsh and bitter, not at all like the Andres I knew. It makes me sad. I've done this to him, twisted him, hurt him, taken his light away. Before I can say anything else he grips my throat, his fingers squeezing so hard that he takes my breath. I know if he flexes his hand any harder he'll crush my neck under his brutal hold. Tears gather in my eyes and I bring my hands up to grip his wrists. He pulls me against his chest and when he speaks he drops his mouth so his lips brush against mine. "You left me, Luna," he growls. "There is only one ending for betrayal."

He slams me against the wall, knocking the wind from

my lungs. My ribs knock against the hard wood. I gasp for air but I can't get any because he's still choking the breath from my body. Just as panic begins to set in and I start clawing for freedom, he lets go. I drop immediately to the floor, coughing and gasping for air. Within seconds I begin sobbing, curling onto my side and crying in terror. Andres steps over me and leaves, slamming the door shut behind him.

10

LUNA

I barely have a minute to pull myself together before he strides back through the door. Maybe if I'd had longer, I would've been up and off the floor, looking for another way out. I know no matter what I do I won't get away from Andres; he's far too big, strong and skilled. But my survival instinct is kicking in. I don't want to die here. I don't want to die at all!

I huddle against the wall and try to stop the sobs spilling uncontrollably from my lips as he walks past me with a couple of bags. "Get up," he growls as he walks by.

When I don't move he transfers one of the bags to his other hand and grabs my arm, dragging my off the floor. I gasp and flail around for balance, half falling against the wall. He doesn't seem to notice or care as he starts walking again, continuing through the house with me in tow. I stumble behind him, exhausted and frightened of what might come next. I lift a hand to my throat, which is sore and bruised.

The house is small and dusty but cozy. It's a bad place to vacation, rustic and seems as though it hasn't been used in a while. Andres drags me through a living room with one big recliner chair, a rug and an ugly picture with a sailboat. Past the living room is a hallway with two doors. He kicks one open and tosses the bags inside. They thump as they hit the floor next to a bed with a patchwork quilt.

I gaze curiously up at my husband. Yet another puzzle. He knew exactly where the candles and flashlight were, and he knows where all the rooms are without searching. He's obviously been here on at least one occasion, yet I've never even heard of this place, wherever it is. A shudder goes through me as I think of the possibilities. Does he use this place for work, to kill people, to run business transactions? Does he bring women here?

Before I get the chance to dwell further he turns on his heel, crosses the short distance to the other door and shoves it open. I glance past him to discover a small but cute washroom dimly lit by a tiny window over the toilet. He pulls me inside, shoves the shower curtain aside and starts the water in the tub. I wrinkle my nose as I realize it's probably going to be ice cold. If there's no electricity, then the pilot light on the hot water heater has probably gone out and I doubt he took the lime to light it. Even if he did there wouldn't have been time for the water to heat.

He turns to look at me, taking in my bedraggled appearance. "Take your clothes off."

I stare at him for a moment, wondering if he's gone crazy. Does he want me clean when he tortures and kills me? Because I'd rather he just get it over with. I shake my head and back away, cringing into myself in a protective gesture. He still has hold of my arm though and he gives it a vicious shake.

"Just take your fucking clothes off, Luna," he snaps. "I'm

not in the mood for this and you don't want to test me right now."

His tone of voice and the look on his face has my fingers flying to the bottom of my shirt. I remind myself that he's seen my naked body thousands of times as I tug the fabric over my hair, wincing when it catches in the long tresses. I reach back to pull at the strands, but Andres yanks it from my hands and untangles them with ridiculous ease, dropping the garment to the floor. A lump forms in my throat as I'm reminded of all the times he's helped hold my hair for me while I changed or brushed the long, unruly mass.

He reaches for the button on my trousers. I tense, my hands landing automatically on his to stop him. I know there's nothing I can do, but I'm feeling protective. I don't know what he plans, but the pit of my stomach tells me it's horrible. I whimper as he pulls the buttons apart and tugs the fabric down my hips, dragging each of the pant legs off my feet with impatient jerks. He makes quick, efficient work of my bra and panties, leaving me shivering, naked and in tears.

For the first time in our marriage, Andres has treated me as though I don't matter. As though my physical body is nothing to him. I've never failed to turn him on before, yet he's acting as though I am just a thing, a nuisance getting in between him and a shower.

He turns his back to me and starts removing his own clothing. "Why are you doing this?" I ask timidly. When he ignores me, I clarify, "I mean why the shower? You obviously can't stand being near me right now. Why are we showering together? L-like we used to?"

He turns around suddenly, a snarl on his lips. I back up so quickly, my hip strikes the vanity with enough force to tear a cry from me. Seemingly without thought, he grabs my arm and steadies me. "Don't fucking question me, Luna."

Heart pounding, fear coursing through my veins, I nod. When he releases my arm, I bring my hands up between us, a gesture of peace and a way to put a barrier between us, even a feeble one. His eye drops to the ring on my finger and he reaches for my hand, grabbing hold of it in a tight grip.

My wedding ring is big and beautiful. Some might call it gaudy, but to me it is perfect. It symbolizes everything Andres and I have together, everything he's given to me. So when he wrenches it from my finger, nearly breaking the knuckle as he drags it from me, my devastation is complete. The fog I've been in since this ordeal began lifts and I'm driven to my knees before the man that put the ring on my finger.

Sobs of animal-like pain erupt from my throat. I have given up everything. I walked away from a beautiful mansion with hand-picked furnishings. I walked away from bottomless amounts of cash, unlimited credit cards and trips all over the world. But worst of all, I walked away from a man that I still love with every fibre of my being. A man that touches every part of me and satisfies my physical body as well as my soul. I did this for my children; their health, their safety and their future. And I failed to save them. Now I have nothing, no children, no husband and no ring. Having the last symbolic part of my marriage torn away from me breaks my heart in a way nothing else can.

He puts the ring in his pocket and finishes undressing. Then he grabs me by the hair and shakes me. "Stop it," he says coldly and thrusts me, still crying, into the shower.

The cool water hits my body, shocking me. I swipe at the tears and try to take calming breaths, shivering under the cold spray. Gradually the sobs die away and the tightness in my chest begins to ease. I cross my arms over my chest, my fingers wrapped around each bicep and I drop my head, allowing the water to rain down over my head. Even cold, it's better than nothing. This is what I do when whenever the world feels like it's closing in, like it's becoming too much for me. I stand in the shower and allow it to wash away my burdens. I cry out my misery and loneliness where only the water can hear. Only Andres knows my secret. He knows that I seek the comfort of water when I'm sad. Did he do this on purpose? Bring me to the shower when I was at my lowest point because he knew it would bring me comfort?

I'm reminded of my mother's death three years ago, the helpless misery I felt as I watched her fade as cancer ate away at her. Each day I would make the trek home from the hospital and climb into the shower, bow my head and cry out my agony and rage. Sometimes my Andres would come sit on the toilet or stand behind me in the shower. He would never say anything. He would simply stay and watch over me, a silent sentinel, there if I needed him.

Just as I begin to soften, begin to hope that he's brought me here to save our marriage, he takes hold of me and spins me around. My head snaps up. I look into his icy, bleak eyes and I remember why he's brought me here, for one reason, he's brought me here for death. This shower means nothing to him. He reads my mind, picking my thoughts through the expressions he's spent years lovingly memorizing.

"Don't," he says, his voice hard and tired.

"Please, Andres," I implore, bringing my hand up to his chest, caressing him the way I used to. "We can talk this through."

He slaps my arm away with such force that I feel something give, something snap in my arm. I scream and grab myself, but he takes hold of both my wrists, swinging me around, picking me up and slamming my back against the wall. He thrusts his leg between mine. I can feel his erection heavy against my thigh. His breath is hot on my neck. I turn my head to see his eyes blazing into mine.

"You could've talked to me a week ago, Luna," he says, his voice quiet, despite the anger I feel thrumming through his muscles. "Instead you chose another, far deadlier path. You stole my entire existence and ran like a fucking thief in the night. For that you will pay."

Before I can respond he takes my lips with his in a brutal kiss. This is not a kiss of passion or love, this is a kiss of pain and revenge, of a man who thinks he has been wronged. This is the worst kiss of my life. He seeks entrance with his tongue and I refuse him. He releases one of my wrists, reaches up and grips my jaw, forcing my mouth open. One of my lips grinds against a tooth, cutting. Blood fills my mouth and I cry out, but the sound is swallowed by his vicious kiss.

I am now weeping uncontrollably in his arms as our kiss goes on and on. I lay against the shower tiles, exhausted and helpless, nothing but a ragdoll. Finally, he moves his face away from mine. I feel a trickle of blood drip down my chin. He shoves his head against my neck and turns his face away as though he doesn't want to look at me anymore. He reaches between my thighs and thrusts a finger inside me, his hand both familiar yet rough in a way he's never been.

My body responds on a primal level, recognizing my husband, the man who has brought me to countless orgasms. But my mind rebels, frightened of this new person who holds me against my will. I'm terrified of my uncertain fate. I can't reconcile the man holding me, fucking me with rough strokes of his long fingers.

"Ahhh," I moan. "Please stop! I can't do this, Andres. Not like this... please!"

"Shut up, Luna," he growls, turning his mouth against my ear. "If I want to fuck my wife, I'll fuck my wife."

"But you're gonna kill me!" I cry out, tears escaping my eyelids even as I feel my traitorous body responding to him, becoming wet, making the glide of his fingers so unbearably good. I can feel myself begin to peak in a way only my Andres can coax from me.

He pulls his fingers out and I start to relax, hoping he's done, that maybe he was just messing around, trying to humiliate me a little. Instead he lifts my leg around his hip, grips my throat and shoves his cock into me so hard my back hits the tiled wall with enough force to knock the wind from my lungs. I gasp and cling to him, dragging my nails down his tattooed biceps as I go weak in his arms.

"If I want to punish my wife," he shouts savagely, throwing his head back, spraying water in an arc. "Then I will do whatever the fuck I want with her."

"Andres!" I cry hoarsely, my voice begging.

He doesn't hear me through his fierce grunts, the raining of the water and the slapping of our bodies. His fingers tighten around my neck and I can no longer utter a single sound. I begin to see black dots and I fight to stay conscious as he takes his pleasure from my body. Tears slip from my eyes, but still I can feel the heat gathering low in my abdomen, beckoning me toward that incredible, mind-blowing bliss.

My bruised shoulders take each strike against the shower wall while he continues to take me higher and higher with jolting thrusts. We've never had sex like this, so rough, so raw, so primal. My hands fall limply from his arms and I lay submissively against the wall taking each hit as pleasure snakes through me like a raging inferno.

Just as I slip into the black void of unconsciousness, my body spasms helplessly in the grip of a deep, dark orgasm unlike anything I've experienced.

I don't know how long I'm out, but I wake up in bed, Andres' naked shoulders hovering over me. I blink a few times to bring him into focus. He's holding my arm, the one that he injured in the shower. For just a second I think I see a flash of guilt cross his sharply handsome features, before he shutters the expression, replacing it with the bleak coldness I have come to expect when the men are working. He gets off the bed and tosses a blanket carelessly over me.

"Don't make more of this than it is, Luna," he says. "We both know how this interlude has to end. You stay here and I go home to our children."

I stay here. As in... I stay here... in the ground.

He walks away, leaving me huddled under the covers of the bed, alone, and once more terrified for my life.

11

ANDRES

Her dark brown, almost black glittering eyes stare up at me like open wounds. She doesn't want to die, she doesn't want me to torture or hurt her. But she made her choice. There's no going back for either of us.

I place her arm gently on the bed, cover her and turn away, leaving the room. I need space from her for a few minutes. Now that I have my wife at my mercy, I'm at war with myself. I want to punish her, fuck her... fuck her up. Break her, hurt her, tear her apart with my bare hands. But even the small amount of damage I've done makes me sick to my soul. Brings back the demons I've spent years chasing away.

I stalk into the living room, stare around for a moment, consider throwing myself into the chair while I wait for her to rise. To come to me with her weak explanations and excuses. But I know I can't be this close to her right now. I'm at risk of finishing it. Of killing her before she gives me what I need. Restitution for destroying my entire world. I will have my pound of flesh before I escort her into hell.

I slam through the door and out into the mid-morning sun. The bright intensity is soothing. We are on a private piece of property off the coast of Spain. I purchased it several years ago when I needed a place that no one else knew about. This is where I come when the darkness of my work gets to me. When I know I can't take it home to my family. I haven't been here in two years though, not since the last time I willingly injected poison into my veins. Not since I cleaned up.

I never thought I'd be bringing Luna here. This place, my hellhole, my sanctuary. I thought maybe one day I'd return and burn it to the ground. Probably still will. Only my wife's body will go up in flames with it.

The conjured image makes me sick. Like a mirage, the vision of Luna twisted and pale in death doesn't solidify. It fades and shimmers into the blue sparkling ocean that I'm gazing at. In its place is a Luna that's healthy and whole, laughing with our children. She's wearing the designer clothes she recently purchased in Los Angeles, big golden hoop earrings in her ears, her ring back on her finger.

I touch my pocket, feeling the shape of her ring, fingering the sharp edge of her diamond through the rough material of my jeans. I can almost smell her, surrounded by a cloud of her favourite perfume, Coco Channel. That pink bottle, I don't remember what it's called.

I stand outside, staring at nothing until I'm calmer. I don't know how long it takes. Maybe minutes, maybe an hour. Sometimes I lose time like that. Disassociate and send myself somewhere else until I'm ready to deal again. It's how I've been coping since the drug is no longer an option.

When I feel ready to face her again, I turn and head back to the house. She's standing in the kitchen when I walk in, looking confused and delightfully disoriented, the way that she does after a heavy nap. Too fucking cute for her own good. I must've been standing outside for a while then. She jumps when I slam the door and turns to look at me, those big, dark eyes wide on my face. Her hair is a riot of honey brown tangles half down her back and half over her shoulder. She's dug through the bag I packed for her because she's wearing the simple pink cotton T-shirt and grey leggings I picked up for her.

A slow burn starts in the pit of my stomach and blood begins to rush through me, headed straight for my dick. She's always made me feel this way, right from the very first moment. Just a glimpse and I want to taste those pouting lips, fuck that delicious body. Our years of marriage have taught me that I'm insatiable where Luna's concerned. There will never be enough time for us.

Annoyed at the direction of my thoughts I snap, "Make us something to eat."

Her lips open to form a perfect 'O', which doesn't help the lustful direction of my thoughts. I can practically read her thoughts as she gazes doubtfully around the kitchen. I sit in one of the hard-backed chairs and slouch with my arms crossed over my chest. I sure as shit am not going to help her. She chose this path, she can walk it for as long as I'm willing to allow. She may as well provide some amusement for me while we're forced into this situation.

She heads first for the fridge, only to find it completely empty expect for an old box of baking soda. The freezer yields similar results. She sighs and closes it softly. Tilting her head to the side she starts going through cupboards, taking stock of everything inside. It surprises me when she finds the pantry and begins rummaging through, mumbling to herself over the limited possibilities. Finally, she settles on a can of soup, a can of brown beans and a juice mix.

She sets each item out on the counter, checks that the oven is gas powered so she can use it, then turns it on. She retraces her steps toward the cupboard that holds the pots and pans. I sit up a little straighter in my chair as she looks for a can opener, finds it and sets to work. She creates a simple lunch for us, but her movements are quick and efficient. All I've ever seen her do in our state-of-the-art designer kitchen at home is create meal plans with our expensive imported Parisian chef and make tea. This is a Luna I've never seen before.

"Where did you learn to cook?" I demand suspiciously as she stirs the soup heating on the stove.

She snorts and tosses me a quick look over her shoulder. "Opening a can is hardly cooking, Andres."

"Never seen you do even this much," I grunt.

She shrugs, turns down the heat on the now boiling soup and moves to the sink to make the juice crystals. "I had to feed myself and mama when she came home exhausted from working double shifts at the factory," she explains, measuring water into the plastic container. She finds a long plastic spoon in one of the drawers and begins stirring. "I didn't exactly learn how to cook gourmet or anything, but I could make simple, filling meals. I had to pull my weight around the house when I lived at home. Jobs were few and far between in that town, so it meant a lot that mama was bringing home a pay check. Cooking and cleaning for us was the least I could do."

I remember the tiny shack of a house that I found Luna and her mother living in when I went to retrieve my future wife. I'd been arrogantly disgusted by the modest abode. I'd wanted to burn it down so she'd never have a place to go back to, but her mother had been sentimentally attached. Instead, I'd taken great pains to show Luna how much better her life would be with me. I'd driven away with her and hadn't allowed her to ever look back.

Now, I remember that Luna had asked for help for her mother. Someone to cook and clean for her. I'd been delighted to give my woman anything her heart desired. But Luna's mama had been a stubborn woman. She'd refused the offer, turning her nose up at a gift from a Los Zetas. I hadn't cared either way, except that her refusal had rankled and I'd limited Luna's access to her mother for a while. Seeing her bustling around the kitchen, talking softly of her mama, I feel a slice of guilt over my actions.

Luna places a steaming bowl of soup in front of me, a plate of baked beans and a glass of juice. When she drifts toward the sink I realize that, instead of eating, she intends to wash the dishes. "Sit," I snap at her back, causing her to jump. "Eat."

The metal spoon she's holding clatters in the sink and she turns to look at me. For a long moment I wonder if she'll defy me and refuse to sit down. I bring my arms up and set them on the table, preparing to go get her and force her compliance. I fully intend to sit her down and force the food down her throat. I don't give a shit about her comfort, I want her to know I'm serious. She will do everything I command, when I command it, without hesitation.

She pauses a second too long. I bring my fist down on the table, causing soup to spill from my bowl, and shout, "Sit the fuck down!"

She jumps, a squeak of fear erupting from her throat. She quickly pours herself a bowl of soup and sits, her legs collapsing beneath her so her ass hits the wooden seat with teeth-jarring force. I smile in dark amusement. This disheveled woman with rings of exhaustion beneath her eyes, no makeup, no jewellery, simple clothing and hair in wild disarray is a side of my wife I've never seen. I wish she was ugly, but I find her just as attractive as ever. Perhaps more so. This Luna is vulnerable, approachable. She looks like she's been freshly fucked. She looks like she's begging to be fucked again; so sweet, so innocent. So in need of another good, hard fucking.

I give my head a slight shake and put my spoon in the bowl, tasting the surprisingly good soup. It's basic canned chicken gumbo, but she's added some kind of seasoning to spruce it up. The beans go oddly well with it and fill my empty belly. I finish my plate, help myself to the leftovers and eat until I'm satisfied. I drain my glass of juice, enjoying the sweet, slightly tart taste.

Only after I've set the glass on the table do I remember that I've hurt her arm. I open my mouth to ask about the injury, but I stop myself. I don't want to give her the impression that I care more than I should, give her hope. She can't build the expectation that our interlude here will end in any way other than her death.

The bleak thought dampens the pleasantly full feeling of our meal. My gaze lingers on her arm, but I can't tell if it's bothering her. Her flawless Latina skin is covering any bruising that might be there and it doesn't look swollen. If the injury pains her then she's hiding it. I shouldn't be surprised. When Cristo was born, she hid her labour pains for nearly two days. I'd been busy with Zetas business at the time and she hadn't wanted to interrupt. She'd known how important my work was. As a result, she'd damn near given birth on our washroom floor all by herself. If one of the maids hadn't found her, she might have bled out and killed them both. But that's my Luna, always making selfish decisions for good reasons.

I'm sharply reminded of other decisions she's made,

other lives she's forced us to take because she can't be trusted. I can feel my chest squeezing painfully as I look at her, innocently sipping at her soup. She doesn't look like the woman that has betrayed me over and over, causing more damage to my life and heart than any other being on this planet. Her nose wrinkles slightly and a look of mild disgust passes over her face. I know that she has accidentally eaten a pepper. She despises them, yet she tolerates their presence in our food because she knows I love them.

I shove my chair away from the table and stand. I ignore her gasp of surprise and turn on my heel, heading for the next room. Once again, I can't be near her. She fucks with my head, one moment inciting me to feelings of murder, the next softening me as I remember her as the woman who stole my heart from the beginning.

I realize almost immediately that by going into the living room I'm trapping myself further in the house with her, with her intoxicating presence. I'm dangerous right now. Unpredictable, like a wild animal. I turn to go back the way I came, out through the kitchen. I'll walk until I'm calm, until I can face her with a certain degree of professionalism. Instead I walk right into her. She's following behind me.

I automatically reach out to steady her, my hands sliding down her supple arms. She flinches a little as I touch her injured arm. Ah, so it does hurt. Fuck it. I shackle her wrist with my fingers and bring her arm up to my face, looking at it closely. Now, this close to my eyes, I can see the damage. It's swollen with the beginnings of a bruise starting to form a few inches above her wrist.

She holds her breath as I examine her, standing stiffly, ill at ease. She fixes her eyes on the floor between us instead of boldly looking me in the face. It feels strange having her look so stiff in my presence. Luna is usually carefree and emotive. She's the first to throw her arms around me and give me a kiss, it doesn't matter who's in the room watching. While I'm glad she understands the severity of our changed relationship, I miss the feel of her against me, her soft curves yielding against my muscles.

I drop her hand. Though I battle internally over the pain I've caused her, there's nothing I can or will do for her. In the end, I'll have to do much worse.

She shocks me when she steps back into my path, blocking me. She brings her hand up to my chest automatically, but quickly snatches it away, cradling it against herself, remembering how I broke it in the shower. I slash her a severe look, but she refuses to get out of my way.

"Please, Andres," she says softly, her eyes still trained on the ground. "Can we talk?"

Though her pose is submissive I feel my ire begin to rise at her presumption. She dares to try to force this conversation? Now, when I'm angry and unstable? I grip her good arm and give her a shake, forcing her eyes to snap up to mine. "You really want to talk about this, esposa? Here? Now?" I ask, spitting out the word 'wife' in our shared language. Fear flares bright in her gorgeous, dark eyes. "You want to discuss why you ran away from our marriage? Why you stole my children from me and put them in danger?"

My voice rises with each accusation and she flinches in my hold, straining away from me. I allow her no escape, no relief from my presence. I jerk her closer, until her breasts are touching my chest. I grit my teeth against the feeling of her peaked nipples grazing me as her panicked breaths make them rub up and down rapidly. I expect her to back down. Instead, she tosses her wild hair over her shoulder, tilts her chin up and meets my eyes.

"Sí, esposo, I do." She stresses the word husband, and

despite my anger I feel some admiration for her daring. Though soft and sweet, my Luna still has a backbone. "There are things you need to know," she says breathlessly, clearly trying to get the words out, but having difficulty. "Things you won't like but need to hear anyway."

I close my eyes for a moment and breath deep, willing the erratic beat of my heart to slow. Telling myself that this is why we're here. I'd wanted an explanation, wanted to see her suffer. Why put off the inevitable?

I release her and step back, shoving a hand through my hair. "Fine, speak," I spit. "Let's get this bullshit over with." Then I pin her with my gaze and point a finger at her, my trigger finger, tattooed with Los Zetas. "But know this, sweetheart. It won't make a difference. You fucked up, and you will pay for it."

She nods and whispers, "I know."

I drop into the lounge chair, taking the only surface in the room and leaving her to stand. I ease back and spread my arms in a careless gesture. "Then speak."

She crosses one arm protectively over her stomach and brings her other hand up to her lip to lick at her thumb, a subconscious gesture. She won't chew on the nail, she doesn't want to make it ragged for the woman who does her manicure. I shake my head and lift my lip in a snarl. It's time to stop noticing these things about her.

"Speak!" I thunder, causing her to jump.

Tears fill her eyes and she stammers, "O-okay." She crosses both arms against her stomach. A tear escapes her eye and trickles down her cheek. She lifts a shoulder to rub it off on her T-shirt. "I mostly left for Cristo."

I stare at her, my mind blank. I don't know what to say for a moment. I try to understand what she means but come up with nothing. Our son has every possible comfort.

Loving parents, loving uncles, an adoring baby sister, more money than he can possibly spend in several lifetimes. What does our son have to do with Luna's selfish choices? It makes no sense.

She must read some of the confusion on my face because she says simply, "He will become a Los Zetas, no?"

And just like that her every action in the past week makes sense. Comes crashing in on me like the thundering of the hell's horsemen. She was protecting our children. From me. From my brothers, his uncles. From the only life Cristo could ever know. My chest aches once again as I stare at her. She sacrificed everything for our son. She did wrong, but she had the best intentions when she did it. And she gave up her life.

A sob leaves her lips as she stares back at me and for the first time in weeks, maybe even months we connect. Shared understanding. She was protecting our son from the life that took my soul, the life that I was never protected from. Not from my parents, not from my brothers, not from anyone but my wife. She is the only person who has tried time and again to pull me from the darkness.

I stand, pushing myself from the chair and walk toward her. She backs up so quickly her back strikes the wall behind her with enough force to knock the wind from her. She gasps and tries to slide sideways, terror now filling her eyes. She's uncertain of her fate. She should be frightened. Her admission means nothing, changes nothing. Except how I feel about what I have to do.

I grip her shoulders, taking in her beautiful tear-drenched face, lift her chin, memorizing every inch of her loveliness. I want to remember her in this moment for all the years to come. This is my woman, my esposa, the mother of my children. My Luna. She has fought bravely for what she believes in.

I drop to my knees in front of her, taking her hand in mine. I kiss the back of her hand, caressing the delicate flesh, feeling her fragile bones against my lips, flexing beneath her skin. She is now sucking in deep breaths of air, trying to fill her lungs. She brings her other hand up and presses it hard against her chest. She looks down at me, her hair a golden-brown swirl tickling the top of my head as I bend to reach into my pocket. I take her ring out and slide it back onto her finger, right where it belongs. This ring is Luna. She lives with it, she dies with it.

I look up at her, finally allowing myself to sink into those eyes, deeper than the darkest night. "You humble me."

12

LUNA

He understands!

Hope flares to brilliant life deep within me. My knees fold and I fall into his arms in an awkward heap. He catches me easily and holds me against his chest, pressing me tight against his heart, his hand at the back of my head. I sob into his neck, clinging to his shoulders. I do everything I've been longing to do. I breathe him in, taking in his familiar scent, loving that he smells like himself, even through so much time away from home.

He rocks me in his lap for as long as I need, until I'm calm enough to talk more rationally. Then, with long, anxious pauses to check his expression, I talk to him. I tell him why I left. "You'd been gone for weeks longer than you were supposed to on that last job, your men had returned but you were nowhere in sight. I... I know you promised you wouldn't touch the drug again, but when I hadn't even heard from you, not even a single word..."

"You should have trusted me, Luna." His voice is hard and I shiver a little. I nod, silently cursing the self-doubts that seem to swamp me whenever I'm left to my own devices. "So what happened? That's not why you left. You said you left for Cristo."

"Sí," I agree, gripping his hand and interlacing our fingers. "I was desperate to know where you were, to make sure you weren't making a mistake, going back on heroin. I tried to call Charlie, but I couldn't reach him. I went to Alberto and asked him where you were, when he thought you'd be back." She takes a quick, sharp breath in. "He told me to mind my own business, that I didn't need to know. When I persisted he grabbed me and tried to shove me out the door. I still refused to go, dug my heels in and started yelling. You know how tenacious I can be. Then I threatened to call Charlie, tell him you were back on drugs."

I can feel the tension run through Andres and he growls, "Luna, you know better...."

"I know," I say hastily, cutting him off. I twist around to look up at him with pleading eyes. "But I would've said anything to get Alberto to talk to me. I knew he knew where you were. You guys are best friends."

"Were," Andres snarls.

"What do you mean?" I ask, frowning, but he shakes his head and shoves his chin forward for me to continue. "Okay... well, when I threatened to call Charlie he was pissed but he knew he had to give me something. So he told me you needed space. Said that you were dealing with the aftermath of the shit you guys'd done on that last job. I... I realized at that point it must've been pretty bad. I didn't want to hear any more so I told him I understood and I tried to leave. He must've been angrier at me for busting in there than I thought because suddenly he was grabbing me, shaking me and yelling about the job, giving me information about things you guys had done. How you'd hunted and butchered a family of four, including ch-children. He just kept talking, telling me all the gory, disgusting details. I couldn't stand it, Andres."

I know I'm talking too much now, too fast, but I can't help it. I can remember the scene clearly, playing out in front of me. "I hit my knees and threw up all over the floor. He leapt back, finally let go of my arm. When I looked up at him he had this smug look on his face, like he was glad I was sick. I think he thought he was somehow punishing me for not knowing my place. For not staying at home and keeping house, waiting quietly for you like an obedient wife."

"Son of a bitch!" Andres explodes and I shudder in his arms as I feel the heat of his anger pour over me.

I grip his arm and try to calm him a little. The story only gets worse from here. "I tried to stand but he came toward me again so instead I quickly crawled toward the door. It was still open, except for the screen. I reached for it and pulled myself up. He laughed and told me to get out, not to bother him again. I ran out the door and straight into Cristo. I nearly knocked him right into the dirt. He'd followed me over there and then stood by the door listening to our entire argument. Dios mio, Andres, I was so upset! I thought he would be stricken by what he heard."

"And was he?" Andres asks, his brows pulling down in a frown.

"No!" The word bursts from me. I feel the ache in my heart and tears forming in my eyes once more as I remember our exchange. "He was simply worried that Alberto and I had been shouting and that I'd been sick. He didn't care about anything else. I even asked him about the family, those children from the story. He said he understood that it was part of your job, that he knew you had to do things like that for work. I asked him how much he knew about papá's work, if there were other things."

"What did he say?" his voice is grim now.

"You know how smart our son is, Andres," I say, my voice flat. "Figure it out for yourself."

His arms tighten a little, but all he says is, "Alberto is lucky he's fucking dead. I would make him suffer for the pain he has caused my family." A chill runs through me as I realize that Alberto has died. I didn't particularly like him, but he was Andres' best friend and second-in-command. He only ever tried to serve my husband loyally. "So you decided to leave," Andres says, inviting me to continue speaking.

I nod, tears clogging my throat. "I had to, this was Cristo's legacy."

"Blood," Andres agrees.

"Death," I whisper.

He pulls me back against him and cradles me in his arms while I let the tears flow free down my cheeks. I speak, finishing the story of our flight. "I didn't want to second guess my decision, didn't want to raise Alberto's suspicion or anyone else's. People are used to my erratic behaviour, so, I left the nanny a note telling her we went on a last-minute shopping trip, went and grabbed Pedro, the only man I knew was stupid enough to betray you, emptied our safe and got us the hell out of there."

"You wanted to save our son," Andres says quietly, pressing his lips against the top of my head.

"Both of our children," I correct him out, swiping at the tears and then clutching his arms. "Sola will marry into this life, she'll watch her own children grow up and become immune to the violence. Cristo will go out, maim and murder. He'll either crave the blood like some men or grow dark and distant. Neither path is bearable for a mother."

"Nor a father," he murmurs.

Yes, he understands.

I slump against him, exhausted, my tears nearly at an end. I don't think I have anything left in me. I am found again, safe in the arms of my husband. Perhaps I'll have to return to the cartel, to the Los Zetas. Perhaps I'll have to go on pretending that this life is acceptable. But maybe, just maybe, one day I'll find a way out for me and my children. I love my husband more than anything on this planet, but my duty is to my babies. I fall asleep in his arms, thoughts of my family firm in my heart.

13

ANDRES

D o it now.

While she's helpless, while she is lulled into a sense of peace. Do what you must before awareness returns with the understanding that nothing has changed.

She sits on my lap, her back pushed against my chest, seeking comfort in the warmth of my body. Her tears have stopped and she's fallen asleep, her breath caressing the hairs on my arm. Her fingers are entwined with mine. Beautiful long fingers beneath my thick, barbaric hand. A hand that has done so much damage.

I lift my left hand and brush the hair from her face and neck. My wedding band glints in the rays of the sun filtering through the dusty window. Luna sighs, a soft trickle of warm air leaving her lush lips and raising goosebumps over the arm holding her head up. I trail my fingers down the side of her neck. Her head falls back into the crook of my right arm, giving me access to her fragile throat, as though inviting me to take the life that must be sacrificed.

Something pricks at my eyes and it takes me a moment

to realize that these are tears. Since leaving childhood I have been driven to tears less than a handful of times. The thought of losing my wife is... unbearable, overwhelming. Life without her feels like a gaping black wound. I know that nothing will be same. As she remains peacefully asleep in my arms, I come to the realization that if we didn't have children, I would follow her into death. I would do what needs to be done, then I would pull out my gun and eat a bullet.

I know what this action would do to my brothers. They would be devastated, angry, vengeful. We are bonded, me and my hermanos. But not even death can separate blood. We will find each other again in the afterlife, wherever that is.

Death can take my Luna. It can separate me and my love. And this is something that I contemplate like a knife to the heart. She is fragile, beautiful, a dreamer. She was never meant for the life that I forced on her. But she dealt with it in the only way my Luna knew how, with dignity and an open heart. She closed her eyes to the ugliness and tried to be the best mother and wife she could be. And she succeeded.

It is her success that will be our downfall.

I wrap my fingers around her throat and close my eyes, counting slowly in my head. When I get to ten I will squeeze. I will crush her fragile neck and kill her as quickly, as mercifully as I can. I tell myself that she will only feel it for a second, that even if she wakes up, she won't know what's happening. That she'll still feel the warmth of her husband against her as he escorts her to heaven.

One. Two.

I clench my teeth to stop the tears, stop my lips from shaking.

Three. Four.

My chest squeezes so hard I can't breathe.

Five. Six.

I flex my fingers out, away from her soft, yielding flesh.

Seven. Eight.

I wrap them around her, pinning her against my chest.

Nine. Ten.

I open my eyes. It's the least I can give her. Watch as I escort her to the shadowed land. I drop my eyes as I clench my fingers. I'm surprised to see that hers are open, her gorgeous velvet, black orbs on my face. I see in their depths, the knowledge of what I'm about to do. She doesn't move, she doesn't lift her hands or fight. She simply lies in my arms, her lips slightly parted, her face angelic and slightly flushed.

"I'm sorry," I whisper, a sob breaking through my calm.

I know, she mouths, unable to say more because I'm now withholding the air from her lungs. I can't bring myself to crush her beautiful, fragile neck. So I simply hold it in my hand and squeeze the life from her. Slowly, her face goes from dusty brown to red. Her mouth opens in a helpless gasp. Her eyes open wider.

I feel something on my face and realize that a tear is escaping. Her arms jerk up, a visceral response to what's happening to her. She clutches my arms, but she doesn't push me away. Instead, she clings to me, pulls me closer, as though embracing me. Her face is now turning white from lack of oxygen and I lose control completely. I cry as I drag her to the floor, my hand wrapped completely around her delicate throat.

Her hands touch my shoulders for a second, drop to my biceps, then fall weakly away, her knuckles thumping against the floor. Her eyelashes flutter. She tries to keep them open, tries to watch my face, those beautiful eyes drinking me in even as they dim. I'm straddling her now, crouched over top of her. My tears raining down on her face, on her chest, on the hand that strangles the life from her.

Finally, her eyes close. Her mouth is open in a tiny 'oh'. Her chest is still lifting in erratic gasps, but they're coming further and further apart. Only a matter of seconds before she's gone. I know that despite my children, I won't live long without her. Maybe a few years. Until I can properly secure their future.

My eyes fall on her face again and then drop further to my hand. I see her name, tattooed on my left ring finger. Luna. I had it done two days after meeting her. I knew from that first moment that there would be no one else in my world. She was it. Luna is everything. My sun, moon, universe. She makes everything better.

I release her, hope and despair clashing and exploding through me in equal parts. If she dies, I die. If she lives, we're fucked.

"Please God, don't die," I beg, my voice sounding foreign, rusty.

I watch her chest, watch her face. After a few seconds colour starts to return, chasing away the pale death mask that had enveloped her, that I'd forced on her. Her chest moves slightly. I lift her hand, bringing it up to my face kissing her palm before pressing it against my cheek. I use her fingertips to wipe away my tears. As her chest begins to fill with air, expanding and deflating with increasing frequency, I move up her body to her head, placing it in my lap. Her eyelashes flutter but she doesn't open her eyes.

"Andres," she croaks.

"I'm here, cariño," I tell her.

She nods slightly and then lifts a hand weakly off the

floor. She drops it immediately, as though she doesn't have the strength to move. I reach out to lift it for her, but she flinches.

"Shh, Luna," I say, trying to keep my voice soft. "I'm not going to hurt you."

"D-dead?" she asks, her voice slightly frantic.

"No, baby," I assure her. "You aren't dead."

She lets out a wail, so sudden and unexpected that I stiffen. Then she curls on her side, rolling away from me on the hard, wooden floor. I feel as though my heart is breaking as I watch her fall apart, even more than when she'd confessed her plans to run away with our children. She sobs and screams out her pain, tearing her already sore throat with cries of despair. I don't know what to do, how to sooth her agony, since I'm the one who caused it. I place a hand on her shoulder and, when she doesn't try to get away from me, run it down her back. This is something I know she loves. She used to ask me to draw pictures on her back when we lay in bed together and she would try to guess what they were.

Finally, as her sobs begin to die away and turn to hiccups, I roll her onto her back. She looks up at me through tear-soaked lashes. I expect to see accusation there. I know I deserve accusation. Instead I see nothing. Just bleak emptiness. As though my Luna has died inside, though I spared her body. I grow cold at this thought.

I push my arm beneath her legs and the other very gently under her back, being especially careful with her neck. I roll her against my chest and stand. I carry her through the house, now growing darker with the shadows of the late afternoon. She lays limply against me, emotionally and physically exhausted. I feel the same, like we both need a week's worth of sleep.

I set her gently in the bed. I'll let her sleep for a few hours and try to find something for us to eat. Then we'll figure out the next steps. Luna can't die. But Luna can't live.

I cover her with the blanket, run my hand over her hair and turn to leave the bed. She grips my shirt, clinging to me.

"Andres," she whispers hoarsely against my chest, clinging to me, digging her nails weakly into my side. "What you did? I understand why, because I understand your world. I knew the moment I left that I was giving up my life." I know the words must be hurting her, but still she pushes on, tries to get them out. "But this is the world I tried to save our son from. The choices I never want him to make." She rolls her head so she can look directly up at me. "If you let me live, I will never stop trying to save him. I will never stop running."

14

LUNA

I wake up alone surrounded by shadows. I bolt upright, clutching a blanket against my chest because I don't recognize anything. Remembrance returns slowly along with aching pain throughout my body, particularly my arm. I'm thirsty but the terrible swollen pain in my throat tells me that a drink will be agony. I push a hand through my hair, fingering the knots from the long strands.

I wonder what time it is. Normally I would check my phone, but that's definitely not an option since I left my phone in Mexico and the burner phone in Cuba. I don't feel very rested or refreshed so I know I haven't slept for long. A shudder runs through me as I think about what Andres did to me. I understand why he did it, but the pain of it is so overwhelming I can feel my mind trying to fold.

My husband tried to kill me. He wrapped his hand around my throat, held me down and squeezed the breath from my body. For those few moments he put his cartel, his brothers, his birthright above me. He put me in my place. *He pulled back at the last moment.* I try to cling to that shred of hope. But I can't help feeling that, while he didn't kill my body, he did murder something inside me.

When I ran from him I knew what I was doing, knew that there would be severe consequences. When I explained to Andres why I ran away I never imagined I would have his support, let alone his love and agreement to my plan. I can't help but wonder if he wishes I'd done a better job. Managed to actually leave with our children, disappear for good. As much as it would have broken his heart, killed his love for me, at least he would have known that we were alive and well. Wherever we were. And that his son, both of his children, were away from the cartel.

After we talked, after he held me and let me cry, I thought... I thought... I don't know what I thought. Perhaps that he would forgive me and we could move on? Be a happy family again. Idiot. I should have known that this would be impossible. You don't fuck over cartel and live to tell about it.

I rub a hand over my face and try not to cry. My face feels raw from crying, like it's been scrubbed by sandpaper. I crawl from the bed, tugging the blanket where it's tangled around my legs and toss it back. I walk slowly to the washroom and flick the light switch. When nothing happens I let out an annoyed sigh. It's clear that this house hasn't been in recent use.

I run the taps and splash water on my face, trying to wake myself up a little more. I dry my face off and squint at the mirror, but I can't see anything in the now dark room. I laugh a little. I've come a long way from the wealthy woman of privilege who had every convenience and amenity at the snap of her manicured fingertips.

I run a hand over my hair and try to restore some order to the wavy mass wishing I at least had an elastic to tie it up with. Andres prefers it down and I usually oblige, knowing I look pretty, framed by the long golden-brown tresses. But now, I think we might be past physical preferences. Still... I feel a little better on the inside knowing I look good on the outside, so I continue restoring my appearance as much as I can.

I return to the bedroom, find the bag that contains some women's items and dig until I come up with deodorant and a toothbrush. I wonder how long he'd originally intended to keep me alive and what he planned on doing to me as I look at the meagre contents of the bag. A shudder runs down my back and I quickly shake off the morbid thought, get to my feet and go back to the dark washroom to finish cleaning up.

When I'm done I find myself standing hesitantly next to the door, clutching the knob with shaking fingers. I'm scared to leave the room, to go to him. How will he act? How should I act? There's not exactly protocol for how a person should behave directly after their spouse tries to kill them. I snort bitterly as I picture myself walking up to him and asking, "Excuse me darling, are you going to try to strangle me again or shall I make us some supper?"

I have a tendency to overthink everything, to analyze every situation and try come up with an appropriate response. Or an inappropriate response, if I'm being totally honest. I know how to use my good looks and emotions to draw a response from the men around me and, in the past, I haven't been shy about using this particular strategy to get my way. I know I sometimes create drama because of this. Now I feel helpless in the face of a situation I can't control. I started this drama by running away from my husband, but I can't control this situation. As much as I want to wail and cry, I know my tears have no place here. There won't be anyone to comfort me through this.

I turn the knob and step into the dim, shadowy hallway. I pause for a moment, listening. I hear nothing but the sound of my own breathing. I think perhaps Andres has left the house to go for a walk, or a drive. Like he did before. Relief flashes through me and I feel a little foolish at fearing nothing but shadows. I continue down the hall, my hand on the wall for support.

I stop short, a cry on my lips when I see him sitting in the chair in the living room. "Andres!" My hand flies to my throat in a protective gesture. There's enough light in the room that I can see he notes the gesture. My heart hammers in my chest and adrenaline floods my system, begging me to run, warning me that this man tried to kill me.

I stand there, still as a statue, fighting with myself, reminding myself that he's still my husband. My knees feel weak and tears prick my eyes. Each breath comes out in a harsh gasp, which hurts my raw throat. I can see that my visceral reaction is affecting him as well. He goes rigid in his chair, his fingers tightening on the arm.

"Come here," he commands sharply, his deep voice cutting like a knife, making me jump.

I cling to the corner of the wall. I feel like I'm going to fall. I have no balance, like I'm in a dream or something. I want to turn and run, dive back into the bed, under the blankets, close my eyes and go back to sleep. But I know I won't make it. He's so much stronger and faster. He'll be right on top of me, crushing me, killing me.

Hot tears slip through, despite my determination not to cry in this moment, to face him without the drama.

"Luna," he says again, his voice just as demanding. He tips the armchair forward so it creaks against the floor, his boots thumping against the hardwood. "I said, come here."

I nod and let go of the wall, forcing myself toward him.

As though I'm marching toward my death, I can feel panic rising. How can he force me to do this? It's cruel, demanding I go to him after what he did to me. I can't stand it.

My knees give out just as reach him and I collapse at his feet, hitting the floor hard. The pain in my legs jars me back to the present, away from the dream-like state I was experiencing. Like a snake, he strikes, reaching out and gripping my arms, dragging me toward him. I yelp and try to lunge back, thinking this must be it. He must've changed his mind. He's about to kill me!

He gives me a little shake. "Stop it, Luna," he snaps. "I'm not gonna hurt you."

Still I flinch back, unable to contain my reaction. My mind is completely at odds with my body. His scent, so masculine with a hint of his soap. His touch. My body recognizes my husband and reacts to him, but instinct, self-preservation begs me to run from him, to save myself. I stay frozen on the floor, kneeling at his feet, my eyes down. "I'm sorry," I whisper, my voice husky and painful.

He drags me toward him until our faces are almost touching, my lips grazing the bristly hairs of his chin where he hasn't shaved in days. His elbows are braced on his knees. "Look at me," he growls.

With extreme difficulty I lift my eyes, past his wide jaw and perfect, sharp features to his blue eyes. They are blazing at me like a wounded animal. A wolf who has been cornered and doesn't know a way out except to fight. My throat catches in sympathy. I know how much he hates the darkness, the terrible side of his job. I despise the idea that I crossed over from being his comfort to another thing that draws him toward the darkness.

I lift a shaking hand and touch the edge of his jaw, running my fingers along the length toward his lips. I savour the feel of his roughness against my skin. This is real, this is my husband. The man that has cherished me for five years. Held me in his arms countless times, given me the gift of his children.

I reach up with my other hand and cup his other cheek before raising up higher on my knees and capturing his lips with mine in a kiss. It isn't meant to be a kiss of passion but one of love and apology. I try to tell him how sorry I am for what I did, for the choices I've forced on him with my actions. But most of all, I tell him that I'm sorry he's not free to live a different life, a life free of darkness, away from the cartel.

When I try to break the kiss, he stops me. His hand goes to the back of my head, cupping me. He crushes me to him, pressing his lips hard against mine, taking what I was offering and then so much more. Andres' kiss is desperate as he thrusts his tongue inside my mouth. When I try to pull back again his other arm slides across the back of my shoulders and he anchors me against him, forcing me to accept his kiss. I taste his desperation mixed with dominance and rising passion. And while my body quickly responds to his demand, like in the shower, my mind rebels.

I can't reconcile our situation. I don't know how this can end. He said he wouldn't hurt me, but for how long? I still betrayed him, betrayed the Los Zetas. Surely there must still be consequences? How can I possibly lose myself in passion while my very life is at stake? With these questions floating through my head I press my hands against Andres chest and push.

He doesn't move, if he even notices my resistance. I try to break his kiss, but he catches me by the back of the head and holds me tight, right where he wants me. He uses his lips and tongue to seduce me into compliance. Andres knows every inch of my body with intimate detail. He has never failed as a lover. Not once have I walked away from our bed dissatisfied. Soon I forget why I wanted away from him. Instead I'm reaching up, clinging to him, clumsily climbing into his lap. He grips me by the waist and lifts me up. Without breaking our kiss he urges me onto his lap, spreading my legs so I'm straddling him.

I wrap my arms around his broad shoulders and fall with him as he leans back in the chair, landing against his hard chest. He cushions me against him, one arm wrapped around my waist, the other coming back up to cup my head. My excitement rises and I rapidly become wet for him as I squirm against the hard ridge of his jeans. His arm tightens around my back, anchoring me solidly against him.

I plunge my tongue into his mouth, bringing my hands back to his face and holding him the way I like him. My kisses are hungry and desperate. Except for our brief moment in the shower earlier, it has been months since we've been together. Andres had been away on business. When he's home we are very active in the bedroom, fucking often and hard. The physical side of our relationship has always been a breathtaking, romantic whirlwind.

I feel his hand clench in my hair and I savour the bite even as I suck on his tongue, controlling the pace of our kiss. We fight for domination in our embrace, me on top, him using the strength in his arms to crush me against him. He pulls at the hem of my shirt and then, without warning, tears it over my head, breaking our kiss. I gasp, rocking back on his lap. But before I can fall he catches me by the back of the head and drags me back to him, smashing his lips to mine. I whimper at the force and then grip him hard, pushing my tongue against his, loving the rush of pleasure that floods through my chest and stomach, straight down to my pussy.

His hands are everywhere, tearing at my leggings, yanking at his own T-shirt. All I can do is cling to him with my hands and knees, try to keep my balance as I kiss his lips, his face and his chest. I lick and nip him every chance I get, every time his gorgeous tanned, tattooed skin gets close enough to my mouth for me to graze him. He groans and grips my head, holding me against him for just a moment, before releasing me to tear at our clothes again.

Soon I am naked, writhing in his lap while he is wearing only a pair of jeans, his cock pulled out underneath me. I reach for it at the same time as I rock forward on his lap, catching him in another passionate kiss, thrusting my tongue against his. His hand lands on top of mine and together we squeeze his penis. Just the way he likes it.

This frantic lovemaking, it feels like coming home, but it also feels different. More desperate. Like we're reconfirming that we're okay. Only we're not okay. Which is probably why we're so desperate to devour each other. To fuck until we can't think. Fuck away our problems. Fuck away the cartel.

Andres wraps one arm around my waist, lifts me and tips me back. "Put your legs over the chair," he commands, his voice rough.

I hurry to comply, opening myself to him. I'd lost all sense of shyness around this man years ago once I'd learned exactly what he could do to my body. Now I am eager for the orgasm I see promised in his glowing crystal eyes. I stretch my legs over the arms of the chair and lean back against his arm, trusting that he will hold me up.

I am barely in position before he's sliding two long, thick fingers into me. In this position we can look each other in the eyes while he does it. I moan, the sound hoarse and strained as he rubs my g-spot with leisurely strokes. I can see so many emotions in his eyes, all forged together through the fires of passion.

"Are you my good girl, Luna?" he asks.

His deep voice, saying those words send shafts of pleasure right through my body. I can feel myself clamping down on his fingers as they continue to pump in and out of my pussy. I'm so wet he has no trouble at all. He uses his thumb to flick my clit in an uneven pattern that drives me crazy. I know he's asking me a trick question. There's no right or wrong answer.

I lick my lips, force my gaze up to his and answer. "I've been a bad girl, Andres."

He nods and I see satisfaction cross his face. He deepens his strokes and I spread my legs even more, rocking my hips in time with his pumping fingers. He rubs his thumb over my clit with increasing frequency. I suck my breath in and fling my head back. I can feel the tips of my hair brushing the floor and I wonder at the incredible strength he must have to be holding me up like this.

"Do bad girls get to come, Luna?" he demands, his voice dropping to a growl.

I whimper as I get closer to my magical peak. But I can tell from his words that he probably won't let me get there. I try to sneak a hand toward my clitoris, but he snaps at me to keep my hands to myself and answer the question. "No, bad girls don't get to come!" I gasp, tears pooling in my eyes. I really feel like I'm going to die if he won't let me come.

"That's what I thought," Andres says, and then leans forward and says against my lips. "But this bad girl fucks me so good I'll let her have it anyway."

He presses his fingers hard against me and rubs my clit furiously while shoving his tongue deep in my mouth. Then he drops his mouth to my breast while I arch back against his arm. He bites down on my nipple, sending me soaring over the edge. Shivers ripple through my body and I shout my ecstasy while I explode in his arms. I can hear him grunting as he watches me fall apart, my hips jerking on his lap, taking everything his fingers have to give. I picture those blue slits, glittering as he stares at me. I love the way my Andres watches me.

He doesn't give me time to recover. He slides his hand from my now soaking pussy, picks me right up off the chair and walks me backward until my back hits the wall. He uses his arm to protect me from the impact, but we still hit hard enough that I feel the wall shake and something on the other side, in the kitchen, falls and shatters.

"Andres!" I cry out, gripping his shoulder with my good hand and trying to get my balance.

He doesn't give me a chance. He yanks my leg up to his hip and slams himself home, sliding deep inside. I gasp, digging my nails into the skin of his shoulders. My orgasm begins to crest again and I lift my other leg, wrapping it around his waist and locking my ankles around his back as stars burst behind my eyelids. I shriek in ecstasy and grind my hips forward just as Andres begins slamming into me. I can tell that my frantic, orgasmic movements are driving him crazy but I can't control myself. He bites down on my shoulder and then slams his hand into the wall next to my head, shaking the whole thing again. I dimly note a thin layer of dust falling all around us.

Suddenly I'm being spun around and Andres is walking with me, then I'm falling. I scream out and wrap my arms around Andres, fully expecting to hit the floor hard, but I don't. My back hits something, jarring me for a second. A quick glance tells me I'm now laying on the kitchen table. As

Andres thrusts back inside me I realize that he moved us so he can go deeper, fuck me harder than he could against the wall.

He cups my head and forces my face up. "Look at me, Luna." I stare up at him, at the intense gorgeous man that loves me like no one else. "Love looking at you, cariño."

"I know," I whisper back and reach up to cling to him, running my hands over his head and shoulders, scratching him lightly, just the way I know he loves. I can feel his cock growing wider inside me and I throw my head back, bringing his head down to my chest, clutching him against me, holding him while he fucks me hard against the table. He finishes deep inside me, bathing me with his seed, warming me from the inside.

After, I hold him close, stroking his naked shoulders until his breathing evens out, which happens far sooner than mine. My throat is very sore and now that I'm no longer flooded with pleasurable endorphins I can definitely feel the pain. Andres leans back on his elbow and strokes his finger gently across the bruises. I can see the sparkle in his eyes dim as his troubles begin to resurface. He rolls off the table and reaches for me. Gently he lifts me and carries me to the living room where he collapses backwards onto the chair with me cradled in his arms.

15

ANDRES

"You've been here before, haven't you," she murmurs, her voice a husky whisper against my throat.

We've been sitting together in silence for nearly a quarter of an hour, naked in each other's arms. I have an excellent internal clock so I can usually tell the time, even when there is no clock available. It doesn't surprise me that Luna is the first to break our silence. What does surprise me is how long it took for her to speak. I stroke the hair from her face in gentle swipes, sifting my fingers through the silky strands. Despite the topic of conversation we are about to discuss I feel completely relaxed, still basking in the afterglow of great sex.

"Yes, I've been here several times," I tell her. "I own this house and the land it sits on."

She nods and I know this revelation doesn't shock her. She's a smart woman, she probably figured out who owned the land as soon as we arrived. Decena men like to be in control of their surroundings. I wouldn't have brought my wife, in such a delicate situation, to a place I didn't have complete control over.

"I've never been here before," she comments.

She's inviting me to lead this conversation. We both know it won't be casual. If she hasn't been out to a property that I own then it's most likely connected to work and related to something I won't discuss with my wife. But she's here now, there's no reason to keep this secret from her. Only this property isn't connected to business. It has nothing to do with the Los Zetas. This is my personal property. No one knows it exists except for myself... and now Luna.

I glance up at a spot on the wall, the bullet hole I drilled through the wood two years ago. "This place was where I came when things became too dark for me, Luna," I say gruffly, tightening my arms around her, holding her lush curves against me, taking in her warmth. "I shut myself in and shot myself up so I wouldn't go home to you, Cristo and our unborn child with the bad things that were in my head." I pause, giving her the chance to speak. When she doesn't I continue, "I knew if I saw you at that time, with that filthy shit in my head that I'd take it out on you. That I'd hurt you... maybe worse."

I grit my teeth, waiting to hear her gasp of shock or anger. Waiting for her to push away from me. I hold her tighter than I know I should, digging my fingers into her rounded hip, anchoring her against me so she can't run away. Instead of the recriminations I know I deserve, she clings to me even closer, pressing her lips against my throat in comfort.

"I know," she whispers. "I've always known why you did what you did... why you took those drugs. But you should've trusted me more, Andres. You should've trusted me to be the one to lead you from the darkness."

I shake my head, leaning my chin on top of her head. She couldn't have chased away the demons that haunted me. That still haunt me. My sweet naïve Luna has no idea what things I have seen and done in my time. The images flash through my mind like a gruesome snuff film on repeat. I've never had the ability to compartmentalize that part of my job, to separate the horrific images from my regular life. They all blend together until I can't tell what's right and wrong. I know my brothers think I'm soft, that I'm too easily touched by the darkness. Maybe I am. I know these past two years have hardened me until I've grown as cold as they are. I thought Luna was my saving grace, the one thing that could still bring me back... until I lost her too.

My gaze lingers on the wall, the bullet hole. I can no longer see it as the room is too steeped in shadows. But I know that it's there. Head height for Luna. The ghost I could never banish; either from my mind or my heart. She has always been entrenched. A part of me, so deeply buried, that it would kill me if I tried to remove her.

She leans back in my arms, her dark knowing look caressing my face. "Can you tell me what it was like?" she asks. Before I can ask her what she means, she continues, "Coming here by yourself. The... the heroin. What was it like? I guess I always thought of it from my own point of view. I knew I hated it... hated what it did to you. I despised how you would come home weeks or sometimes even months after a job, weak and sad. You were a different man from the husband I knew. It took you ages to get back on track. But I want to know what it was like for you?"

I look down at her face, now shrouded in shadows. I touch a tear that threatens to spill from her bottom lash and rub it between my thumb and forefinger as I consider her question. This is very introspective for my Luna. She is a wonderful, smart woman that is capable of great feelings of love. But ultimately she is a selfish woman, doesn't look too deeply into the thoughts and motives of others.

However, she seems to truly want to understand. And though I despise the idea of bringing Luna into my dark, disgusting world of addiction, I think we need to take this step together. Perhaps she should know. I nod and stretch, pushing the chair so it inclines back, holding her in my arms so she's forced to sprawl on top of me. She snuggles against me with a shiver. We are both naked still and though summers in Spain are warm, a chill is beginning to set in as fall nears.

"I used to fly here after particularly nasty jobs," I tell her. "So I could be alone. I wasn't fit to be near anyone, let alone you and Cristo."

"Where exactly are we?" she asks softly.

I hear the hesitation in her voice. She knows she is pushing boundaries by asking, but she's desperate to know. I consider telling her but decide against it. I shake my head. "I'm sorry," I tell her. A shudder runs through her body and she stiffens against me. I feel a catch in her breathing where her breasts brush my chest. I realize what she thinks and curse my own stupidity. "No, Luna, it's not what you think. I promise, I'll never hurt you like that again." I tilt her chin so I can look into her eyes, promise her with words as well as without. "Doing what I did to you... it was like tearing out my own beating heart, impossible. I just can't. But for now, we're still at an impasse. Until I decide how to proceed, it's safer for you if you don't know where you are."

She frowns but doesn't disagree. "Okay, Andres. I trust that you know best." The stiffness gradually melts from her limbs and she snuggles back against my side. I run my hand along her curves. "Please continue."

I hold her tight against me as I talk, staring down at her, reminding myself that I'm here with Luna, not back in another time. "It was the best, most wonderful thing I've ever experienced. Nothing, and I mean *nothing* compares to the feeling of heroin speeding through my veins." She makes a sound and I know she doesn't like what I've said. It doesn't matter. She wanted to hear the truth and this is what I give her. "I came here to forget everything. Forget the people we hunted and tortured. The women we ordered our men to brutalize, rape and dismember." Her breath catches and her nails dig into my side. I understand. She knows what cartel is about, but the details are brutal. This is what she was trying to save our son from.

"I understand," she whispers. "You needed to forget the things you saw."

I shake my head and stare down at her, wanting her to really understand. "The things I did, Luna. Don't pretend I'm an innocent, I'm not. I'm a weapon. I do as I'm ordered. I get told to hunt and kill, then I fucking do it." Tears glitter in her dark eyes turning them to onyx. "I came here to forget everything. The cartel, my brothers... even you."

"Me," she repeats, her voice catching.

"How can I do my job with someone like you in my head?" I ask, a hard edge to my voice now. "How can I purge that shit with you still in my head? I think about you constantly. You're my everything, but I can't do what I have to do while you're constantly there. So I came here, slammed as much of that shit as I could until I forgot every-thing, until I turned numb."

"Did it work?"

"No," I admit, running my thumb over her collarbone,

reminding myself that she's real. "You were always here. You've never truly left me."

I can see the glitter of her white teeth flash as her lips stretch in a quick grin. "Good." I don't mention the time I shot her ghost trying to banish her from ruining my high. Something tells me she won't like that. "But you were always clean when you came home?"

The way she says it is part question, part statement. "Yes," I run my hand over her, touching her breast softly. "After Charlie pushed me to sober up, showed me how, I started doing it on my own when I came out here. I'd go on a bender, fuck myself up until I thought I could manage my own thoughts, then I'd force myself to clean-up."

"How did you do that?" she asks curiously, innocently.

I shudder, unable to hold my reaction back. The images flash though my brain, almost as bad as the hideous things I've done to my victims. Didn't have a choice though, I'd inject the heroin until I was out. Then I had no choice but to detox. The debilitating pain of sobering up is almost indescribable. My body would bend until it nearly broke, shivering, shuddering, purging, essentially dying, until it rid itself of the toxin. This would last for days, sometimes up to a week. I would lay in my own filth until I was once more coherent enough to crawl to the washroom.

Perhaps the withdrawal is what I wanted, even more than the drug. After my brother forced me off heroin the first time, I discovered absolution in withdrawal. There is no judge or jury in my line of work. I have only myself as a moral compass. I know I do things that I will regret, things that will put a black stain on my soul for the rest of my life. The pain of withdrawal is the closest I can come to death without maiming myself or committing suicide. It brings me comfort in the sea of disgust I feel for myself and the things I have done.

Instead of explaining this to Luna I kiss the top of her head and murmur, "Let's get something to eat."

She nods and tips her head back so I can kiss her lips. She understands that this topic of conversation is closed. "I think I saw another soup and a couple cans of peaches in the pantry," she says, crawling off my lap.

She reaches back to catch my hand and leads me from the room that holds too many ghosts.

16

———

LUNA

I t's morning and we've been here for a full day. I still don't know where *here* is. Andres has left to pick up groceries and other supplies. While he's away I decide to go for a walk. I pull on a fuchsia tank top and a pair of white shorts that show off my tanned legs. I find a pair of cheap floppy sandals in the bottom of the duffel bag and pull them out. They have those plastic things that go between the toes. I make a face, deciding grimly that Andres really must have been planning on killing me because no way would I have worn these unless I had no other choice except death.

I smile and stretch my arms wide, welcoming the sun as I step out the front door. My problems feel as though they melt away in the warmth that touches my bare skin. Most of our family and friends think that we named our daughter Sola because my name is Luna, because she is the sun to my moon. This is only partly true. We named her this way because I have always been a worshipper of the sun, because she lights up my life and brings sunshine to everything around her. How can she not? She is innocence.

I feel an ache in my chest as I think of my daughter. I'm reminded of why I'm here, that my future is still uncertain. So far, I've tried hard not to think of my children. I've vacationed often without them and they've been fine, more than fine, in the care of their excellent nanny. There is no reason why this separation should be any different. Andres and I will fix things and then we'll go back to our children.

I wander as far from the house as I dare, which isn't very far. First, I go to the edge of the cliff and then around to the driveway. I walk up the road, but I don't want to lose sight of the house so I turn back before reaching any main roads. I shade my eyes, one hand on my hip and turn around in all directions but I can't see any other people or houses. Just tall, baked grass and a few scraggly trees. I think about climbing down the cliff where it's less steep to walk along the beach but I'd noticed driftwood on the sand indicating the tide comes right up to the cliffs. Unsure what time that would be, I decide against this plan. Besides, if Andres comes back and finds me missing he would freak.

So I return to the house and set about dusting the layers of grime from all the surfaces. I shake my head at the lack of furniture and personal touches. The place reminds me of Andres' home at The Site before I moved in with him. It was sparse and uncomplicated, like him. A smile twitches my lips as I remember our first months together. He'd given me carte blanche with his credit cards and flown me to some of the best cities in the world for shopping. When I'd gotten over my initial shock, I'd done those cards justice, sending shipment after shipment of purchases back to the house. After seeing what I'd done to Andres' home, several of the Los Zetas wives asked for my decorating and fashion advice, which, of course, I was happy to give. If I hadn't married Andres and settled down as his wife, I do believe I could have become an interior decorator.

My mind whirls as I consider the possibilities in this humble home. How I might decorate it if given the opportunity. I frown and shake my head. No, I must not think that way. This isn't my true home and it never will be. Although it has promise as a cute little vacation cottage if Andres will allow me to make some major changes.

"Luna!"

I jump as I hear him come through the door, shouting my name. I drop the cloth I was using to dust and hurry to meet him in the kitchen. I frown when I see the amount of groceries he's carrying.

"You can start putting these away," he tells me without looking up as he dumps them on the table. "I'll get the rest and then start working on the electrical problem, see if I can get the lights working."

My mouth goes dry and I stare after him as he shoves the door open. "The rest?" I say faintly. How long are we staying here?

I automatically reach for the nearest bag and pull it toward me. Tears fill my eyes as I start to empty the bags. It becomes quickly apparent what Andres has done. He's bought enough food for an army. An army of one. A single person who loves strawberries, avocadoes, taco fixings, burritos, beef stew, beans, apple pie... all canned and frozen.

My breathing grows shallow and black dots swim across my vision as realization strikes. He intends to leave me here. Alone. I lift my eyes to meet his as he kicks the back door open. He stops in his tracks, his face reflecting my discovery. I can see the truth written there and I know I'm right.

"Luna..." he says, his voice pleading as my knees give out and I hit the floor.

I'm not trying to be dramatic, but I can't seem to stay standing. I reach out and grab one of the table legs so I'm holding on to something as he drops whatever he was holding and rounds the table, reaching for me. "Don't touch me!" I snap as his hands land on my shoulders.

He ignores me, pulling me away from the table and curving me against his chest. "Luna, baby, I'm sorry," he says against my hair.

His words break me and I start crying. I don't want to cry. I want to be angry at him. I want to stand up. I want to shout and throw groceries at him. Toss cans of beans and peas at his head while screaming how much I hate him; then he'll say he's sorry and we'll have passionate make-up sex underneath the table. That's what the old Luna would have done. But I don't do that, because I know this scenario won't end that way. Andres won't take me home. Because he can't.

I soak his T-shirt with my misery as I cry for my children. I hurl insults at him, tell him I hate him for what he's doing, call him a monster for separating a mother from her children. Then I switch tactics and start begging. I lose all dignity and promise him anything and everything if he'll just take me home. His arms tighten in sympathy but I know he won't weaken.

"My babies!" I scream as I beat my fist against his shoulder. "You fucking bastard."

I can feel his tears landing on my head and I know he's hurting as badly as I am. We cry together until I run out of tears. I curl on the floor with Andres at my back, his arms firmly around me. I don't want his touch right now but I'm too weak in heart and body to shove him away. For the first time in my life I think I understand the lure of drugs. I would do anything to feel numb. As my sobs turn to slight catches he speaks, tries to explain his plan to me.

"You betrayed me, Luna. And by betraying me, you betrayed the cartel," he says, kissing the back of my neck. "This is an undeniable fact. I may forgive your action, I may understand why you did what you did, but it won't ever go away. You can't go back to your life the way it was. You should be dead right now." A tiny sob escapes my throat before I can call it back. I tip my head into the floor pressing my cheek against the wood. He keeps touching me though I don't want him to. "I can't kill you and I won't allow anyone else to do it. So I'll do the next best thing. I'll keep you here, hidden away, forever."

"My babies..." I croak, my voice breaking.

"Dead to you," he says, his hand tightening on my waist. "You made your choice knowing what would happen if you were caught."

The tears begin to fall again, sliding steadily down my face, soaking the floor, though no sound escapes me now. The pain is so great I feel as though my heart will explode. "No," I gasp. "I won't do it. This is worse than death!"

He tangles his fingers in my hair and forces my head back. "You don't have a choice, Luna. It's this or death and I won't fucking kill you."

"Then I'll kill myself!" I scream out jerking violently in his arms, trying to hit him. He refuses to let me up. "The second you leave me alone I'll slash my wrists! I refuse to live here alone, without my children... without you."

He holds me against him, his arm tight around my waist, his hand still in my hair. He speaks in my ear, trying to make me listen to sense, but I won't hear it. "You'll have me, when I can come out here, a few times a year," he says, his voice aching with grief. "Just not the children."

"No!" I scream, struggling, throwing an elbow into his

stomach. I hear him grunt. "Fuck you! I swear Andres, if you leave me here I'll kill myself the second you leave!"

He goes rigid beneath me and for a split second I believe that I've won, that he won't leave me. That he'll take me with him when he leaves, that he'll think of a way to take me home to my family. Then he's flipping me onto my stomach with him on my back. I screech in pain as he lands heavily on top of me, my ribcage slamming into the unyielding floor, the breath whooshing out of me.

"Andres!" I yell, choking on my own tears.

He grips my hair in a fist and yanks my head back while I try uselessly to crawl out from underneath him. He places his lips against the shell of my ear and growls, "You won't hurt yourself if you have a child."

I freeze as my brain scrambles to understand his meaning. Will he bring me my children? No, his family won't allow it. Take me to them? But that doesn't make sense, he said he won't do that. Then he quickly follows his words with terrifying action, until I know exactly what he means. He tears my shirt from my body, heedless of the welts he raises on the skin of my shoulders. His anger is so great that his actions are both passionate and violently angry.

"No one fucking hurts you," he shouts as he rises over my back. "Not you, not my men, no one but me."

I yelp in shock as he yanks the little white shorts right off my hips without unbuttoning or unzipping them. My body jerks in reaction and I curl underneath him, breathless in anticipation, eyes wide in wonder. One moment I'm crying my face off with heartbreaking loss, the next I'm being mauled on the kitchen floor. Only moments ago I wanted a drug to numb my mind and body... well this is it. And I don't have to do a thing.

I feel my bra snap as Andres tears the strap from my

back, pulling it away from me. I cry out in reaction, but not in denial. If I could I think I would roll over and embrace him, take him in my arms, wrap my legs around him and beg him to fuck me. But he's too heavy. He's right on top of me, holding me down, pinning me to the floor, grunting his pain and anger in my ear as he shoves my legs apart with his rough jean clad thighs. I cry out as my tender skin drags across the floor, but I savour the sensations too.

"I'll give you a child, Luna," he says, dragging me to my knees.

Then I realize exactly what he means. He doesn't mean my children. Not my Sola or my Cristo. He means a new child, a different child. And it's a possibility, I haven't taken my pill in two days, not since running from Cuba. I scream and cry out, try to lunge away from him, but he's holding me too tight. I try to twist around, to strike out at him. I manage to hit him in the side of the head as he's unbuckling his belt and readying himself. I drag my fingernails down his tattooed arm and am gratified to hear him swear viciously. He clamps the same arm tight around my middle, dragging me back against him until I can barely breath.

"I hate you!" I scream, hitting the floor with my fists.

"I know," he grunts as he enters me, sending me soaring.

I cry out as I'm flooded with feelings; relief, pleasure, pain, terror, they all crash through me in a maelstrom of emotional and physical sensations. I'm bombarded, I'm wrecked. I can do nothing but hang on as Andres slams into me, violently, ruthlessly, relentlessly. Soon I'm sobbing as he takes me higher and higher. Instead of fighting I'm clinging to his arm like it's a lifeline instead of a bind. Tears are coursing down my face, hitting the floor. My cries have turned to passion, his hoarse grunts mingling to fill the air.

We're in tune once more, though we've never been farther apart than in this moment.

I can feel him flaring wide within me, lighting up every pleasure centre with fire until I feel as though I'll become an inferno. I widen my legs, inviting him to touch. He knows, understands my invitation. He reaches beneath me and rubs hard, flicks and then pinches my clit. I throw my head back and scream as he bites down on my shoulder, marking me. Incredible, unending, blissful pleasure rushes through me as he empties himself inside with each thrust.

We collapse together, him on top, pinning me to the floor once more, his hand tangles in my hair. His head is on top of mine and our breaths mingle together while we struggle to come down from that explosive high. Tears fill my eyes once more and my shoulders start to shake. I think he senses rather than sees my emotion.

"I'm sorry, baby," he whispers against me.

He's going to leave me here.

17

ANDRES

I look down at my sleeping wife where her head rests next to my hip and take another sip of my tequila. I skipped the shot glass and poured myself a nice big tumbler after Luna cried herself to sleep. She refused to allow me to hold her, offer her comfort. Only after she fell asleep did I cover her with a blanket and sit next to her, smoothing my hand over her lush curves. She's so exhausted she doesn't even notice my touch as she slumbers.

I wish there was another way, but I know there isn't. She's too much of a loose cannon. She can't be trusted. She's fucked up too many times. If she does anything else stupid, does it around Charlie, Nic or the Los Zetas, her life really will be forfeit. Which means my life would be forfeit as well. Because this moment in our lives, this desperate snapshot, has taught me that Luna really is my anchor to this life. I am nothing without her. If she dies, then so do I.

I'll go to my brother, tell him she betrayed me, stole my children, fucked me over and ran away with that pendejo, Pedro. It kills me to dirty her name like that, but I'll have to make my family believe that I killed her. Believe that I was angry enough to destroy her. Won't demand her body as proof.

I use my finger to swipe the hair away from her face. I want to see the gorgeous features that I fell in love with and stayed in love with over these past years. She is everything to me. She has held my heart in the palm of her small hand since the first moment she lifted those bottomless moon-filled eyes and looked into mine. She pierced me that day and every day after. Even the days we weren't together, she was still in my heart, still stabbing away at me, reminding me that she was always there. I was never alone.

I can't stand the thought that I'll leave her here. Alone. She'll hate it. Luna is a social creature. She's bright, she's fun, she's everything that I never was until I met her. She made me so much more. And now I'm forced to let her go. Because she made the right decision. Because she wanted better for our children than the life of the cartel. And she failed.

I drain my tequila and stand, dropping the empty glass on the dresser. I pull my T-shirt over my head and toss it in the corner, then take the phone from my pocket and set the perimeter alarm before climbing in beside Luna and allowing exhaustion to claim me. I haven't slept in days, maybe even weeks. Perhaps things will seem better tomorrow. After all, I still have my wife, she'll live, even if she's not happy.

18

LUNA

I wake up feeling warm, surrounded by the familiar scent of my husband. For a moment, just a single moment, I think we're back home at The Site, our children just down the hall in their rooms, the nanny in hers, the cook about to prepare breakfast. As realization hits, a spike of pain pierces me and it's everything I can do not to throw Andres' arms from my body. I try to keep my breathing even so I don't wake him up.

My mind is racing. He intends to keep me here, forever. He wants to take me away from our children. I understand why. Or at least I'm trying to, but it hurts so much. He thinks giving me a new child, one that his family doesn't know about, will solve everything. I don't want a secret child. I want Cristo and Sola. I want my babies. They fill my mind until they're all I can think about; their sound, their smell, everything about them. I lay next to Andres obsessing about my babies until I become consumed by my thoughts.

I think hard, trying to figure out what to do. I'm not stupid, but sometimes I make bad decisions. That's what got me into this mess. Think, Luna, think! How can you get your babies back without putting a bullet in your skull or getting yourself stranded in this fucking bullshit badly decorated, dusty cabin in God knows where?

Then it hits me. When he dropped the groceries, he also dropped the car keys. After he fucked me on the kitchen floor we both picked up the groceries, but I grabbed the keys and tossed them on the counter next to the coffee pot. At the time I was too numb, too emotionally drained to think anything of it.

My heart picks up as I turn my head on the pillow and look at my husband. His sharp features are clearly outlined by the moonlight filtering in through the window. For the first time in over a week I can feel the anger, fear and anxiety draining from me as I see my next course of action clearly outlined before me. It'll probably end in my death, but seeing my babies one more time, holding them in my arms, kissing them, is worth my life.

I touch Andres, skimming my fingertips over his slumbering features. He doesn't move, doesn't sigh, nothing. I touch his mouth, his firm but gentle lips. They've given me so much pleasure, both in words and actions. I twist around and press my lips to his, hoping I won't wake him. As I pull away my eyes fall to the angel stamped across his shoulder, her hands lifted in prayer. I send a quick thought her way, asking her for guidance, begging her to send me safely back to my children as I slip from the bed.

I don't bother with a sweater or shoes... nothing. I wear only a long, thigh-length T-shirt and panties as I run swiftly through the house expecting him to wake up and come after me, grab hold of me and drag me back at any moment. Follow through on his threat to keep me here, impregnate me to keep from committing suicide, never let me see Sola and Cristo again. I slap a hand over my mouth to cover a sob as I make my way down the darkened hallway, clinging to the wall when I trip over the edge of the rug.

I nearly cry out as I slam into the kitchen table, bruising my hips against the wood. "Ay, dios mio!" I whisper savagely into the darkness, screwing my eyes shut against the pain. I suck in a breath and listen for movement in the hall indicating I'd woken Andres with my clumsiness.

When long seconds pass and I hear nothing, I feel my way around the table to the counter where I know I tossed the keys earlier. My heart leaps into my throat as I feel around. I'm forced to blink tears from my eyes as I squint, trying to see in the dim moonlight as I search. Fuck, I can't find a damn thing! As I'm about to give up, decide that they aren't here, my fingers land on them, right next to the sink. They must've been shuffled over somehow. Maybe when we were unpacking the last of the groceries.

I grab them and lurch toward the back door, my hand landing on the handle. The breath catches in my chest and I stop, my fingers freezing in the motion of pulling the handle. I bow my head, thoughts flying at lightning speed. I didn't think I had any tears left but I was wrong, they splash down my face as I stand motionless until I'm driven to my knees.

I see everything in a flash of images, like a photo album, or a movie, playing through my head. My marriage, a hasty event, just me, Andres, one of his brothers and my mama. But I was so fucking happy. Because I knew I loved him, that I was going to love him forever. Then there's Cristo... I tried to hang on, tried not to let anyone know how close I was to the birth. I knew Andres wanted to be there, but he was away on business. And then he wasn't, then he was there, right there with me, by my side through the whole thing as I gave birth to our son.

Next our daughter. Sola was just as hard as Cristo. Fuck anyone that says the second child is easier. They're wrong. Andres refused to leave me for that whole last month of my pregnancy, wouldn't leave my side. Told his family and anyone that would listen to fuck off if they dared to talk to him while I was so close to birth. Every time she kicked he was rushing the doctor to me, convinced I was about to pop. When Sola finally came, he was on his knees by my bedside begging the good Lord to spare me the pain, then he was on his feet threatening my doctor if both me and the child didn't come through the delivery okay. It was everything I could do to convince him to shut up, calm down and hold his newborn daughter once she finally came into the world. In her own time, like her mama.

And now we're here, a broken family, not something I ever imagined a possibility. But I refuse to go out of this life without ever seeing my babies again. They came from my body, they belong to me. I will touch them once more... after that Andres and his family can decide what to do with me. I refuse to stay here, isolated, living a lonely life. Wondering, imagining, hoping, aching, for my loved ones. Impossible.

I stand up. I open the door. And I start running.

I had wondered if the house was wired, electronically monitored. I got my answer the moment I reach the car and unlock it, flinging the door open.

"Luna!"

My head jerks up as Andres hits the edge of the door frame, bellowing for me. He's lurching, his mind still fragmented from sleep, but having been quickly wakened from some kind of alarm when I fled from the house. I know I don't have much time. This is a man used to making snap decisions. A man that kills without blinking, with only seconds notice.

I leap into the car and slam the door shut behind me. I have enough presence of mind to hit the door locks, but I nearly freeze when I see him start running across the yard toward the car. I scramble to jam the key in the ignition but scream and drop them when I feel the car rock. I don't look up, instead reaching down to grab the keys again. I think he hit the hood of the car with his fist and now he's moving toward my window. I manage to fit the key back in the ignition and turn it despite my severely shaking hands. He tries my door just as the engine turns over.

"Fuck, fuck, fucking motherfucker," I mumble. My dear departed mama would be appalled if she heard how badly my language has deteriorated this week.

"Luna!" he roars. "Open the door."

I'm shaking, I'm panicking. I know that next he will try to shatter the window. I don't know if he'll succeed. My heart feels like it's going to burst from my chest. I grab the gearshift and throw the car into drive, hitting the gas. Only I don't put the car into drive. Somehow, I've put it in reverse. I rarely ever drive on my own and I'm too upset to slow down and check what I'm doing. When I hit the gas the car lurches backwards. I scream as my body is slammed back in the seat by the force.

"Luna, stop!" Andres shouts.

I barely look up at him, too frightened of what I'll see on his face. He'll kill me for sure after this stunt. Why do I make such stupid decisions all the time? Maybe I should've just stayed in the house, waited until morning and tried to argue him into taking me with him. I've had Andres wrapped around my finger for five years. I could have convinced him to take me with him. Now he'll never relent. He'll never trust me not to be impetuous and stupid.

"Idiota, Luna!" I growl at myself, slamming my foot on

the brake. The car skids backward in the dirt, lurching and then tipping. I don't know what's happening. I finally look up. Andres is standing next to my window again. Except his face doesn't reflect fury... he's terrified.

"Luna..." I see his mouth form the word, but his voice doesn't penetrate the window. I don't understand. I don't know why the car is still moving backwards even though my foot is no longer touching the pedals. I twist around in the seat to look behind me but I can't see anything but darkness.

Yet the car is definitely tilting sharply. Then it hits me. The cliff. I've driven too close to the cliff and the car is starting to slide over. That's why Andres stopped banging on the widow. He doesn't want to accidentally push the car right over the edge. I frantically twist back around to look at him. I see despair written all over his face and I know the car is seconds from going over.

"Seatbelt!" he bellows.

His single word galvanizes me and I reach for the safety belt. But it's too late. My fingers grab hold of the material, yank at it, just as the car tips wildly. I fling my head up to look at him, look at my husband one last time as I go over the edge. He opens his mouth, says something, maybe screams it, but I don't hear over the rushing in my ears.

Then I'm flying, my body free floating inside the car as it falls through the air. I try to catch sight of Andres one more time, but the car has moved, maybe flipped over as it falls. I feel a second of jarring, bone-crushing pain.

"Andres..." I whisper, hoping he doesn't do something stupid, like follow me into death. Our children need him.

I feel something wet touch my face and I wonder if the tide is still in. Then nothing but the comforting embrace of darkness.

19

ANDRES

Buzz, buzz, buzz...

I wake up, instantly alert, my hand hitting the bed next to me. Fuck, she's gone. I know exactly what's happened, though I pray that we aren't under attack, that Luna hasn't been taken somehow. Impossible. No one knows about this place. She's left, trying to get back to our children on her own. If she manages to get off the property she could easily be taken by an enemy if she makes a wrong move, if she's detected in a place she shouldn't be. All of us Decenas have targets on our backs. Luna knows this, but she's desperate, exhausted, hurt. She might make a mistake.

And once she's home, if she says the wrong thing to the wrong person, her life will be taken. She's too emotional to think clearly, she needs me by her side, tempering her reactive nature. I should have tied her to the bed. Shouldn't have slept so hard. Shouldn't have had that tequila. I should have known she'd run the first moment she had a chance. Our children mean everything to her.

All this runs through my head in the split second it takes me to leap from the bed. I grab my phone, hitting stop on the perimeter alarm. I run for the door, hoping I have enough time to get to her. I silently promise that I'll do whatever it takes to negotiate with my wife, to somehow make this situation more acceptable. Maybe when the children reach eighteen years I'll explain everything, bring them to her. They can cry and reunite. She'll hate this option, but it's a sliver of hope in a bleak situation.

I fly down the hall and around the corner to the kitchen. I see the back door is open and sprint for it, glancing around for the car keys. My hopes are dashed though when I make it to the door, pausing to glare out into the yard. I can see her clearly in the moonlight, opening the car door and sliding into the driver's seat.

"Luna!" I shout.

Her head pops up for just a second, but then she ignores me and slams the door shut. Even though I can't hear the locks I know she's smart enough to have engaged them the moment she closes the door. Fury rushes through my system as I start sprinting across the yard. She better fucking have locked that door, because once I get my hands on her I'm going to beat her into next week. After I convince her to get out of the car. Convince her to negotiate with me.

I can see her fumbling to get the key in the ignition, but her whole body is shaking. I don't want her to be able to start the car, she's in no shape to drive. I slam my fists on the car, hoping to scare her. She nearly jumps out of her skin and I see her mouth open in a shriek, or a sob. Grim satisfaction rolls through me as she reaches toward the floor where she must've dropped the keys.

I fling myself around the side of the car, reaching for the door frame. I'm going to have to shatter the window. Just as the thought runs through my head she starts the car, revving the engine.

"Motherfucker!" I snarl to myself, banging on the window, then louder, "Luna! Open the door! Don't you dare drive away."

My anger turns rapidly to icy horror when I see her fumbling with the gearshift. "No, baby, no," I beg, banging louder on the window, trying to get her attention as I see her put the car in reverse. I glance toward the cliff, a grim shudder going through me as I see how close to the edge I parked the car. She has no fucking idea what she's doing. "Fuck!"

The car lurches backward and I can do nothing but hang on and beg her to pay attention. "Luna, stop!"

She twists around, her wide eyes trying to figure out what's happening. Then she does exactly the wrong thing, jamming her foot down on the brake too hard, sending the car into a skid in the loose dirt. The back tires catch for just a second and then the car starts to slide on its own, tipping. I can already tell by the angle that the fucker will go over in a matter of seconds. I leap away from the window not wanting to make it go any faster.

I stare at her, our eyes connecting. Hers are flooding with panic and, finally, understanding. "Luna... I'm so fucking sorry. For everything," I say grimly, not loud enough for her to hear. And then my brain kicks into gear. I know I can't get her out, but maybe I can make her a little safer, make it so she can somehow survive the disaster to come. "Seatbelt!" I yell.

My gorgeous girl reaches for it, but she's too late. The car flies up, clipping me hard in the shoulder with the side mirror. I'm thrown to the ground as it goes over the edge. I crawl to the cliff and watch in disbelief as the car flips upside down and lands with a splash on the surf below.

"Luna!" I yell, tears stinging my eyes.

I don't wait, I don't try to find an easier, less steep path down. I start climbing. I realize quickly that my shoulder is so badly bruised it's nearly useless. I'm forced to cling to the cliff, slide and grab with my one good arm. I grunt in pain as I jar my shoulder. I don't dare look down. I don't know how high the tide is. What if the car is sinking? What if it's already under? What if she's drowning or drowns before I can get to her? What if she died in the impact? I know the odds aren't good that I'll find her alive. It's at least a thirty-foot drop.

As I near the last ten feet I finally glance over my shoulder. I can see the car. It's either floating or the tide isn't very high. Either way, I take a risk and let go of the cliff face, jumping into the murky water below. At first I'm enveloped by cool water, embraced, then I hit the sand as my legs reach the bottom. I'm jarred, but not injured. I surface quickly and realize I can stand. The water is only chest deep for me when the waves hit and knee deep as the tide goes out.

I turn and make my way quickly to the car, terror filling my heart with each sodden step. The car seems to have landed upside down on some rocks, the back tilted up. I take a deep, gulping breath and drop to my knees in front of the windshield, which still faces the cliffs, where it's most protected from the oncoming waves. I crawl underneath, swiping water from my face and I squint into the interior of the car, my hand on the glass. At first I can't see her, then, as the waves recede once more, I see her.

"Luna," I whisper, feeling my heart shatter. She's laying on the ceiling of the car in a pool of water, her hair floating around her. Her arms and legs are thrown in every direction and her head is tilted back. She isn't moving.

I hit the windshield with my closed fist as hard as I can. It vibrates beneath the pressure but doesn't break. I know if

I hammer it hard enough I will break it, but I'll risk breaking my hand as well and with a bruised shoulder I'm already in rough shape for carrying Luna out if she's still alive.

It damn near kills me to leave her alone in there, for even a second, but I need to think smart. I leap away from the front of the car and head to the base of the cliff dropping to my knees. The water is relatively warm as it hits my bare back. My jeans are completely soaked now and stuck to my thighs and waist. I search until I find what a need, a decent sized rock.

I carry it back to the car, and though I don't want to lose sight of my girl, I know I won't have enough leverage to smash the windshield where the car lays. I carry the rock around the side, lift it over my head and shatter the passenger side window. It only takes one hit for the entire thing to shatter into pieces and fall. I drop the rock and clear the glass.

Without pausing, I crawl through the open window, ignoring the scream of pain in my injured shoulder. The second I'm through I reach for her. I stop though, my hand hovering over her still face. I don't want to hurt her more by being careless, by moving her when I shouldn't. But I can't fucking leave her here either.

"Luna, baby," I whisper brokenly, finally dropping my hand to her cheek and touching her.

She feels warm. I close my eyes for a second and then drop my fingers to her throat. I'm swamped by fear, but I know I have to find out if she's alive. I nearly weep from relief when I feel the steady beat of her pulse against my rough fingertips. Never in my life has it been more important for me to feel the lifeblood of another human being rushing beneath my touch.

Next, I lean over her, placing my head above hers, my

ear over her lips. I hold my breath as I wait to feel hers. I can feel my heartbeat pounding against the wall of my chest as the seconds tick by. At first, I fear that she isn't breathing. That I'm too late, that I made a mistake and she's dead. But then I feel the delicate rush of her breath against my throat, familiar and warm. She's alive. I know I shouldn't move her without checking her limbs for further damage, but I'm overwhelmed by emotion. I gather her in my arms and hold her against me, thanking God that she survived the fall.

"Okay, baby, we have to move," I say against her head. She doesn't respond, not that I expect her to. I finally do the smart thing and check her limbs for damage. I don't see any obvious breaks besides her slightly swollen wrist, which I'm pretty sure was already broken from our time in the shower. I'll save my guilt for later. For now I need to get us out of the car before it turns into a watery grave. I can't be sure if the tide is on its way in or out or that the car won't shift and sink beneath the surf. Anything could happen to turn our situation even more perilous.

I pull Luna as gently as I can through the broken window, careful to protect her from the edge of the windowsill. A small moan escapes her lips as she falls into me, her legs dangling over my arms, her bare feet touching the waves beneath us. I stare down at her, watching for any hint or flicker of life, but she remains unconscious.

I look up at the cliffs, judging the best place to carry her up. I don't know what kind of damage she's taken, why she's unconscious. I don't want to risk throwing her over my shoulder and scaling the sheer face in case I do even worse damage to her head. I walk through the water as quickly as I can until I reach a part of the cliffs that are less steep and start climbing. I do my best not to jar Luna as I carry her, but the going is tough and I'm trying to move quickly.

As soon as we reach the top, I lay her out on the ground and check her out again, this time going over her more carefully. I feel her head and realize that she has a sizeable bump on the back. I pray there's no brain damage, that she'll wake up from this healthy and whole. As I run my hands over her body I think maybe there's some damage to her ribs as well, but I'm no doctor so I can't say for sure. I'm usually the one doing the breaking, not trying to fix it.

Hands shaking, I reach into my pocket and pull my phone out. Thankfully it's in a protective waterproof case. I dial the local Spanish emergency number and wait for someone to pick up.

LUNA IS in a coma for five days. The first two are from the knock she took to the head, the last three are medically induced, to give her swollen brain time to recover. This morning the doctor took her off the meds that were meant to keep her under. She's now on some serious painkillers for the cracked ribs, broken arm and twisted ankle.

I am beside her, waiting for her to wake up. I snap at a nurse as she speaks too loud, touches Luna too impersonally, telling her to leave the room after she checks the intravenous drip. I want to tear all the shit from my wife and walk away from the hospital with her cradled safe in my arms. I hate being surrounded by unknowns where we can be picked off, easy targets.

My family has already stepped in with the local law enforcement, smoothed things over for the most part. I didn't have much explaining to do. As far as the cops are concerned Luna was in a car wreck trying to run out for ice cream at 3:00am when she accidentally put the car in reverse. Luckily, the noise of the car crash woke me up and I was able to climb down the cliffs to rescue her. They didn't question anything, simply writing the accident off as a wealthy woman with very little driving experience.

Luna's doctor raised some concerns. He saw the finger marks around her throat, guessed that some of her injuries hadn't come from the car wreck. He hadn't wanted me in the room with her, but I wouldn't be moved. I coldly informed him that we are on a second honeymoon and enjoy certain types of sex. My tone of voice did not invite further questions. And in the end, my power and family spoke louder than his desires.

Soon my brother will arrive. He intends to stay until Luna wakes. Or... if she doesn't. He wants to be here whatever comes, supporting us. I need to talk to her, try to get through to her before he arrives. I pray that she can hear me. Somehow, I have to believe that she can.

I take her hand in mine and squeeze her fingers, stroking the skin of her arm with my other hand. I imagine that I feel her fingers twitch in my hold, tickling my palm softly. I lean close and whisper in her ear, "Luna, mi amor, you must listen to me. Your life depends on this. We took the children to Havana for vacation but decided to send them back home to Mexico with their nanny. Then you and I came here to Spain for a second honeymoon...."

20

LUNA

I can hear something beeping and it annoys me. I hear voices talking in hushed tones, then a man's voice raised in anger. I hear sneakers squeaking on the floor. Cool hands touch my arm, poke and prod me. These things all annoy me. I'm pretty sure death shouldn't be so fucking annoying. The beeping, the hushed voices, everything, they all suck balls.

I want to say something. Open my mouth and tell them all to fuck off. To bring me my sun chair and margarita. I earned some tasty booze, I earned heaven. I tried to be a good mother and wife. I tried to be the best! Maybe I was a failure, but it wasn't for lack of trying. I died trying to be the best I could be. I earned better than this annoying bullshit, whatever this is.

It takes me a few hours... or maybe a few days, I'm really not sure since I can't seem to open either my mouth or my eyes, to figure out that this isn't heaven. Thank God! I'm probably not even dead. Death shouldn't suck this much. Awareness comes to me in flashes, sometimes vague and floaty, sometimes sharp and painful. Like broken movie clips.

I finally realize that I'm in a hospital. Which makes perfect sense. That means I didn't die at the bottom of that cliff. Somehow, I was rescued from the wreckage of the car. I hope I'm not too disfigured. I laugh internally, because I still don't seem to have control of my body. I know it's a shallow thought, but I really don't want to be ugly. I don't have many skills. I'm vivacious and pretty, that's what I'm known for.

But then... I realize, Andres will love me no matter what I look like. He's not shallow. He's amazing and incredible. I wonder what kind of drugs I'm on. Morphine maybe?

The only thing that doesn't annoy me in all this floaty bullshit is a scent, a smell underneath the sharp sterile hospital scent that overrides everything. It's comforting, it's Andres. He's always there with me, floating through this awful nightmare. He never leaves. Sometimes he's touching me, holding my left hand. Sometimes he's just nearby, snoring softly. For a long time, perhaps days, he doesn't say anything.

Just when I think he's so angry that he's stopped speaking to me, he picks up my left hand again and he squeezes it. I try to squeeze back, try to tell him I can feel him, that I'm here with him, but I'm too exhausted to make my fingers work. He'll just have to trust that I know he's there. I smile internally when he leans close, his scent rushing over my face. I can feel his lips brushing my ear as he speaks.

He says, "Luna, mi amor, you must listen to me. Your life depends on this. We took the children to Havana for vacation but decided to send them back home to Mexico with their nanny. Then you and I came here to Spain for a second honeymoon. You were restless, couldn't sleep and wanted a midnight snack. You decided to leave, even though you should've known better. You accidentally put the car in reverse and you don't remember anything after that. This accident happened because you sometimes make stupid, impetuous decisions." I hear his voice catch and he stops speaking for a moment. His hand tightens on mine until the pressure is almost too much, but I don't think he realizes. His voice is deep and firm when he speaks again. "You were badly hurt, baby. These bad decisions, they have led us to this moment. I will take steps to ensure this doesn't happen again, that I have your compliance, but you will have to help us both by being a good girl, by being the best. You must never step out of line again. All of your free passes have been used up. You understand?"

Yes, I understand. He can't protect me forever. If he's not around to step in for me again, then someone else might. His family, the Los Zetas, someone else less forgiving than the man who's hopelessly, irrevocably in love with me.

I know that now is the time to connect, to reach for him, so I gather as much strength as I can and I open my eyes. At first, I can see nothing except streaks of bright lights stabbing my fragile vision. For one horrible moment I think I am dead and I got it all wrong, but then I blink a few times and squint my eyes. Gradually things come into focus. I can see a TV in the corner of the room, a table, a door. I look to the side and I see my husband bent over my arm, his forehead touching the back of my hand, as though he's praying over me.

"Andres," I whisper.

His head snaps up so fast I nearly get dizzy with the movement and if I had enough energy I would smile at the look of disbelief and delight mixed on his face. Relief slides through me as his eyes fill with tears of emotion. He's happy that I'm awake.

There are so many things I want to tell him, that I love him, that I need him, that I'll never betray him again, but I don't have the strength. And I suspect I don't have enough time. His family will arrive soon. Instead I try to tell him this wealth of information in just two words when I whisper, "I understand."

He studies my face for long moments. I don't know exactly what he sees. I try not to think about what a mess I must be. Finally, he leans over, smooths the hair off my forehead and kisses me. As I drift back to sleep, a feeling of peace settles over me. Nothing has changed. My husband is still cartel, I am married to cartel and one day our son will become cartel, our daughter will marry into cartel. But all of this...? Is it out of my control.

EPILOGUE

ANDRES

Six months later

"Mama!" Cristo and Sola throw themselves into Luna's arms as she hits her knees in the dirt outside our home at The Site, heedless of the damage she's doing to her silk trousers. I think she said they were Valentino or something. I don't usually pay attention to the brands unless they're sexy enough that I want her to do a little extra shopping.

I chuckle as she lands kisses all over their faces, tries to answer the questions they're peppering her with while pulling gifts from the bags she's carrying. I know they will notice me in a few minutes once they get over their initial mama obsession. Though we passed off that late night mad dash Miami boat ride as a vacation, the children know better. They felt the tension, the fear. They remember Luna's tears, her cries as they were being hauled away. Cristo is particularly protective of Luna now. He watches her like a hawk and becomes grumpy when she needs to leave for more than a day. He was unbearable the days leading up to this recent vacation when he learned that they wouldn't be accompanying us.

Luna and I went on a real second honeymoon. She decided she wanted to go back to that house in Spain. I didn't understand why, thought it would have too many traumatic memories. Thought if we were going to do anything we should burn the place to the ground and then spend the rest of our trip in Mallorca. Instead she'd decorated the damn place, purchasing ridiculous amounts of furnishings online and having them shipped overnight. My wife proved that if you throw enough money around you can have anything shipped anywhere in a truly impressive short period of time.

Once she redecorated the house in Spain it looked completely different. Even the land felt less barren after I'd walked it daily with Luna at my side. She would chatter incessantly in her sexy, slightly husky voice about ridiculous, unnecessary things while I fell a little more in love with her. This was the first time since her accident that I felt like I had my beautiful girl back. True to her word, after we'd returned to Mexico, after her stay in the hospital, she'd become a model wife and mother. She didn't put a single toe out of line. To my eyes she became so subdued that my heart ached for the old Luna, the woman with moonshine in her eyes and mischief in her smile. I don't think the difference was detectable to anyone but me though. It was a relief to get her alone in Spain, where we could be ourselves once more.

My ulterior motive in taking Luna away from The Site was to have her outfitted with a tracking device by a doctor known only to me. Of course, there's always a chance that word could get back to my family. If this happens we'll tell them I was worried over her safety, that I want to know where she is at all times in case she's ever grabbed. Unfortunately, in our line of business we have enemies, and Luna does enjoy her shopping trips and vacations. But in reality, I will now be able to track her every movement. I will know the moment she's in a place she's not supposed to be.

I remember explaining the procedure to her. I flew the doctor into a private clinic in Spain where he met us. I thought she would finally crack, finally lose her temper with the restrictions I have piled on since our time in Spain, since her flight with the children. But she didn't say a single word.

She simply sat silently through the procedure, her eyes dimming a little more. I could read her thoughts, feel her hopelessness for the future. Later, when we got back to the house there was an edge of desperation to her. I could feel her need to be alone, sink into her grief, but I wouldn't allow it. She belongs to me, even her despair is mine. She resisted when I pulled her into my arms, turning her face away from me, pushing her hands against my chest.

I gripped her chin and forced her to look at me. Her dark eyes glittered with defiance and I grinned savagely down at her. This is the woman I want, the passionate, vivacious Luna that I fell in love with the moment I saw her. Even if I can't have her all the time any more.

"Do you love me, Luna?" I demanded. There could be only one answer to my question, we both know it. Still, when she hesitated I tightened my hold until I knew it hurt, knew her excitement was increasing with mine. Since our explosive time here our sexual encounters have grown darker, edgier.

"Sí," she finally snapped, her face reflecting her rising passion and anger. She reached up and grabbed my cheeks, dragging my head down to hers. Against my lips, she whispered, "You are my everything, Andres."

THE END

Thanks for reading. I hope you've enjoyed **LUNA & ANDRES.** If you could leave an honest review on your retailer and/or Goodreads, I'll be forever grateful.

If you are reading this book somewhere other than through Amazon, my other titles will become available within the next year, starting September 2019. Thank you for your patience during this transition.

Happy reading!

Nikita

Book Eight - Burning Beauty (Coming 2019)

The Driven Hearts Series

Book One - Driven by Desire

Book Two - Thieving Hearts

Book Three - Capturing Victory

The Sanctuary Series

Book One - Sanctuary's Warlord

Book Two - Sanctuary on Fire

Book Three - The Last Sanctuary (coming soon)

Standalone books

Because You're Mine

Mine to Keep (a novella)

Stalked

After Dark

In collaboration with Jasmin Quinn

Collared: A Dark Captive Romance

Safeword: A Dark Romance

Chained: A Mafia Marriage Romance

Good Girl: A Captive BDSM Romance

Hostile Takeover: An Enemies to Lovers Romance (coming soon!)

Visit *nikitaslater.com* for more information

and the latest updates!

STAY CONNECTED WITH NIKITA!

Don't miss one sexy moment. Keep in touch with Nikita for the latest news and updates about all of your favourite characters.

- Follow me on **Amazon** for all of my book releases!
- Follow me on **Instagram**
- Like and follow me on **Facebook**
- Follow me on **Twitter (@NikSlaterWrites)**
- Connect with me on **Goodreads**
- Follow me on **Bookbub**!

Sign up for the newsletter today at receive exclusive updates and access to *bonus content and chapters* not available anywhere else!

www.nikitaslater.com
nik@nikitaslater.ca

ABOUT NIKITA SLATER

Nikita Slater is the International Bestselling dark romance author of the Fire & Vice series, Angels & Assassins series, The Queens series and several standalone novels. Her favourite genre is mafia romance, the bloodier the better, though she loves to write about every subject under the sun. She lives on the beautiful Canadian prairies with her twelve-year-old son and two crazy awesome dogs. She has an unholy affinity for books (especially erotic romance), wine, pets and anything chocolate. Despite some of the darker themes in her books (which are pure fun and fantasy), Nikita is a staunch feminist and advocate of equal rights for all races, genders and non-gender specific persons. When she isn't writing, dreaming about writing or talking about writing, she helps others discover a love of reading and writing through literacy and social work.

LUNA & ANDRES derives from **Anita Gray's** International Bestselling, **The Dark Romance Series.**

Blaire is "Compelling Dark Romance," says Anna Zaires, New York Times Bestselling Author

"Screen worthy," says the BestSellers & BestStellars Book Blog

All titles in **The Dark Romance Series** are available with Kindle Unlimited and as Audiobooks.

To find out more, *Click Here*